The Baseball Bat

Learning to Control Anger and

Anxiety with Help from Gramps

James Shaw

**This book may be ordered by contacting
James Shaw, PsyD, at <u>www.drjshaw.com</u>.**

Cover design by Jonathan Correll
Layout by Savannah Correll
Edited by Savannah Correll; Jacquelin Nguyen, MD;
James Wickman, MBA

Because of the dynamic nature of the Internet, any Web
addresses or links contained in this book may have changed
since publication and may no longer be valid.

ISBN: 061589030X, EAN-13: 9780615890302

Printed in the United States of America

Disclaimer: The information, ideas and suggestions in this
book are not intended as a substitute for professional advice.
Before following any suggestions contained in this book, you
should consult your personal physician or mental health
professional. The author shall not be liable or responsible for
any loss or damage allegedly arising as a consequence of your
use of application of any information or suggestions in this
book.

Author's note: This book is a work of fiction with the
exception of historical facts and locations. Names, characters
and incidents are the product of the author's imagination or
are used fictitiously. Any resemblance to actual events or
persons, living or dead, is coincidental.

To my daughter, Stephanie,
whom I watched hit homeruns as a young girl,
and have watched as she has hit it out of the
park as a wife and mother.

Contents

—✦—

Baseball Sign-ups...1

In the Beginning... 11

The First Practice 21

Anger Control 29

Neighborhood Game................................... 37

First Game 43

The Machine.. 53

Flipping Out 61

A Glance... 69

Focus on Grades.................................... 75

Low Times...83

Better Times 91

Creating Calm... 99

Start of Summer 107

No Guts, No Glory.................................... 117

Fireworks 125

"Every day I get in the queue,
(too much, Magic Bus),
to get on the bus that takes me to you
(too much, Magic Bus)."
— The Who (1968)

Baseball Sign-ups

I t was Wednesday, March 20, 1968.
I had just gotten off the bus from Twin Beach
Elementary School. The school was over a
mile from my house, which meant taking the bus
was my primary means of transportation. I was in
the fourth grade. I still had two more years at this
school before heading to the junior high. The bus
dropped us off on the south side of my street,
Pontiac Trail, as usual. Getting off the bus with me
were five other neighbors; all of them were in
lower grades than me.

After looking both ways, I dashed across the
street without waiting for any of the other
neighbors. Since it was Wednesday, I first headed
to the mailbox to check if *The Spinal Column*, the
local newspaper, had arrived. Then I walked to
Carol's house, just two doors over from mine. My
mother had arranged for Carol to watch me until
she got home from work. I didn't really think I
need watching. At 10-years-old, many times I
would just check in with her and go to my own
yard. I had the world figured out as much as any
adult, or so I thought at the time. I knocked on
Carol's door to let her know that I had made it
home from school safely. Since she had to watch
her own two pre-school boys, she didn't mind me
wanting to play outside.

1

After cutting through the yard that separated Carol's house and ours, I took out the mail and sat on our front porch. I leafed through the paper and found it! There it was, the article for the annual Lakes Athletic Association baseball signups! I could hardly sit still and wait for my mother to get home, so I could convince her to sign me up for baseball. Impatiently waiting for her, I daydreamed about how I would hit homeruns and make plays in the field. For Christmas, I had asked for a first baseman's mitt, a baseball bat and a Pitchback Net and got all of them. I was determined to play first base this season.

I didn't realize it at the time, but I had already developed a very over-confident personality. In other words, I had quite big dreams and didn't think for a minute that I might not achieve them all. I had to be over-confident because after my disastrous first season, it was quite clear my thoughts certainly weren't realistic.

My first season of playing baseball was a year ago, when I was 9-years-old, playing in the Mustang League. Many of the other boys had already been playing for a few seasons, and the team consisted of 9 and 10-year-olds. Before starting the season last year, I had hardly ever swung a bat, thrown a ball or caught a ball. I had gone to the first practice with a plastic glove, and the coach had written me off as the last hitter in the lineup. Each game I played my required two innings in right field. I did not have much success throughout the season. I struck out almost every time I was up to bat and only felt *some* success when the umpire called a ball instead of a strike and *great* success every time I made it through stepping up to the plate to bat without being hit by the pitch.

During one of the games, I heard some parents laughing at me. One father even went as far as to say to me that I wouldn't know where to run if I did happen to hit the ball. This angered me a lot, and I growled that of course I knew which way to run. I sat on the bench and thought a lot about what he had said, and then I started to watch the game. My first thought was to watch very carefully for anyone who did hit the ball to see where they ran. After watching a few players run to first, I breathed a sigh of relief that I did know where to run. I committed to memory that when I do hit the ball, I will run and run hard to first base. My thoughts then turned to how I would be teaching this guy a lesson some day when he would see me playing for the Detroit Tigers.

You might think that after my first season of baseball that I would certainly not want to sign up for baseball again, but the total opposite was true. I wanted to play very badly and prove to everyone that I could be the best player. The Pitchback Net was a pitch-and-catch device with a steel frame and a net, so that when I threw the ball at it, the ball came back to me. Using this device was how I learned to throw and catch. It didn't matter if there was six inches of snow on the ground; I was still out there throwing the baseball against the net and catching it when it came back to me. I didn't learn to play catch with friends as typical boys did. As I threw and caught balls against the Pitchback Net for hours, I envisioned myself being successful and making plays in the game.

I also learned to hit the ball by throwing rocks up in the air and hitting them into the woods. My mother had rocks spread over the driveway to prevent it from getting muddy when it rained. She knew I was hitting the rocks into the woods, but she never said anything or tried to get me to stop. I let my imagination run wild, picturing myself hitting a homerun as the rock sailed high into the woods or seeing myself racing for a double when I hit it lower. Needless to say, the bat took a beating and was so badly chipped that it could not be used in a real game.

—◆—

When I saw my mother pull in the driveway, I was still sitting on the porch. Before she could even open her car door, I shouted, "Mom, I got the paper and can sign up for baseball."

Somehow, I was so excited that I didn't even think to greet her with a hello. My mother could sense my excitement, so as soon as we got inside, she looked at the paper.

"Mom, I want to sign up. I'll be one of the older kids on the team this year, so I'm going to be one of the stars."

My mother replied, "Yes, Tom, you can sign up for baseball."

She would only agree with me, but there had to be some doubt inside of her after watching me play last year.

Then my mother greeted me and asked about my day. My day? I couldn't think of anything but baseball.

"Tom, I'll take you to every practice and every game. Do you have any homework?"

I had a social studies assignment, so I told her that I had some homework. She didn't criticize me for not doing the reading before she got home like many parents might have done. She let me succeed or fail on my own. I didn't do my reading that night because I was too excited about baseball.

My mother asked what I wanted for dinner and I replied, "We better call the league first; the teams might be filling up." I might have been hungry, but signing up for baseball was more important.

"Oh Tom, I'm sure they have room for you. I'll call, but then we need to have dinner."

My mother dialed the number from the paper and someone answered. "I would like to sign my son up for baseball. His name is Tom Mochina, pronounced Mo-shee-nuh, and he is 10-years-old as of February this year." She then gave the person on the phone our address and phone number, and then she turned to me and said, "They want to know what position you play."

"First base. I play first base!"

"First base," she said as she listened for a while, took a few notes, and then hung up.

I was lucky. They could have asked what position I played last year. Instead, they asked what position I play, and now I play first base. I had a first baseman's glove to prove it.

"Mom, what did they say?"

"Tom, they are going to call us and tell us when the first practice is going to be after they get teams assigned."

"Thank you for telling them first base and not right field. I was worried you might say that."

My mother just smiled and then asked if I wanted hamburgers for dinner. After eating, I watched *Bewitched* and then *Batman* on our small black and white television. *Batman* was my favorite show and it was on both Wednesday and Thursday evenings. On Wednesday, it was the first part of the weekly episode where Batman and Robin would find themselves in some kind of danger; then on Thursday, they would find a way to escape and catch the villains.

The next day, I got on the bus for school still daydreaming about how well I would do on the baseball team this year. A couple of boys were horsing around and one of the boys bumped into me, apparently after being playfully shoved by the other boy. My thoughts immediately turned to how dare he bump into me. He should know better than that. What is wrong with this boy? I need to teach him a lesson. I shoved him away from me without saying a thing. The boy hit the seat and fell to the floor crying. I could feel my heart racing as I just sat there staring straight ahead. The bus driver stopped the bus to attend to the boy and asked what had happened. The boy pointed at me and said I had shoved him.

As the bus driver looked at me, I said, "I didn't do anything. These boys were horsing around, and one of them got hurt."

Apparently, the bus driver didn't believe my story and gave me a warning that if I were involved in any more trouble on the bus, I would have to go to the principal's office. Since the principal knew me well from getting into a lot of trouble last year, this would not be good for me, so I just sat there, heart beating rapidly and holding my tongue, staring downward.

For the first two or three hours at school that day, I was still feeling angry and didn't talk to many people. I tried to smile a lot, but when something like the bus incident happened, I didn't smile for most of the day. By lunchtime, I was feeling better and talked to my friend Mike during recess when we were on the playground. I asked him if he signed up for baseball and he told me that he didn't know it was time to sign up. As it turned out, Mike didn't want to sign up for baseball. We walked around the playground and looked at the girls. There was one girl that had caught my eye. Her name was Valerie, and she was short and thin with short brown hair. None of the boys in my class had girlfriends, but if someone admitted to liking someone, then people would say she was your girlfriend, even though in most cases the boy hadn't actually talked to her. I kept my crush on Valerie quiet.

Mike wasn't one of the biggest boys, nor was he extremely athletic, but he was my friend and we got along well. Some of the more athletic boys were engaged in a game of kickball. The top athletes in the fourth grade were Stan, Will, Marty and Joe. They seemed to do well in all sports. They often bragged about how they excelled in baseball last season. They all lived close to the school and were all on the same team last year. They were known as the "walkers," and I had to ride the bus since I lived a mile away. There was status in being a "walker." Marty was the self-proclaimed strongest kid in the class. He and I scuffled a year ago when he told me he was the best fighter in the school and I told him that I was. Somehow, I just couldn't let anyone be better than me at anything. Actually, I was a pretty scary fighter because I got so angry that I would stop at nothing to prove my worth.

On Thursday, April 4th, when I got home from school, I checked in with Carol as usual since my mother was working. She was watching her small black and white television similar to the television we had. She told me that Martin Luther King, Jr. had just been shot. The only time I had seen a black person other than television was at the Pontiac Arby's. There were only white people at my school. I know this would seem racist today, but it was the reality that we lived with back then. There were no other races of people in the school. The only thing that I knew about Dr. King was that he had given the "I Have a Dream" speech, where he wanted equality for all, which I agreed was a very good idea. I watched how sad people were at the news of the assassination. That evening, I watched the speech by Bobby Kennedy, who was next in line to be the President of our country, to officially announce the death. I wondered if I was safe in this world or if someone would try to shoot me some day. I know I should have been mourning the death, but I was worried about myself. In the weeks following the assassination, there were race riots in Detroit, which I thought were too close for comfort.

A few weeks after I had signed up for baseball, I was home eating dinner with my mother when the telephone rang and my mother answered, "Tom, it's for you."

I grabbed the phone from my mother and said, "Hello?"

The voice on the other end said, "Tom, this is Coach Franciszek. You are going to be on the Cardinals this year. Do you have a pencil and paper?"

I recognized that last name as the same name as Stan's, so his father would be my coach and I would get to play with boys from my school. Last season, there were no boys from my elementary school on my team.

"Give me just a minute," I said, scrounging for something with which to write. "I'm ready."

"Good" said the coach. "Our first practice will be at Twin Beach Elementary at 6:00 p.m. on Tuesday. Will you be able to make it?"

"Yes," I said, dreaming about how successful I would be during the season.

The Baseball Bat

"What's your name?
Who's your daddy?
Is he rich like me?
Has he taken any time,
to show you what you need to live?"
— The Zombies (1968)

In the Beginning

W hen my mother was very young, her parents emigrated from a small Protestant, Hungarian town about 40 miles from Budapest. My mother and her parents settled in Ferndale, Michigan, where her father worked in one of The Dodge Brothers' factories (which later became known as Chrysler) to make a living. According to my mother, my father's parents also emigrated from Hungary and settled in Ferndale where his father also worked for The Dodge Brothers.

My mother and father met in high school and began dating. They went to movies and dances together. They even talked about getting married, but when my mother found out she was pregnant, she told me that the news was too much for my father, and he decided to leave her.

I didn't really think about my father much. I wondered sometimes why he had never come to see me. Every year before Christmas, my mother and I would get a Christmas card from my father with a check for $20 with a note that simply read, "For Thomas." My mother then used his return address to send a card back with a current picture of me and a little about how I am doing which only

11

included the positives aspects of my life. Last year she wrote, "Most people now call him Tom and he is doing great in school. He does very well in math, English, social studies and spelling. As you can see, he is becoming a very handsome young man. He has taken an interest in music and sings very well along with radio. He is also becoming very athletic and runs about constantly. Helen." She graciously left out any trouble that I had gotten into and some of my low grades.

We lived with Grandma and Grandpa Mochina until the summer before I started kindergarten. My mother worked as a dispatcher for a trucking company and Grandma stayed home with me. I don't have too many memories of this time, but I can remember two experiences, both relating to my uncle. He once scolded me for taking one bite out of several cookies, which I cleverly thought would claim them as mine. My mother had often told me if I touched the food, I had to eat it. I can remember another time when he was holding me and not letting me go. This feeling of being trapped felt horrible to me at the time.

My mother was very involved in a Methodist church in Ferndale and she had developed some good friendships. One of her friends mentioned that her parents were selling a little house out in West Bloomfield Township and suggested that it would be a good purchase. After seeing the house and the community, my mother, at the age of 23, decided that it would be a good decision to buy this house as a place to raise her son. She thought it would be good to move from the city to the country (even though today, this area is considered part of the Detroit suburbs). She was able to buy this very small two-bedroom house with one bath, one living area and a kitchen with a loan from her father.

Although the house was very small, the property was bordered by a wooded area to the West and North, which belonged to the property owners who had lakefront houses on Upper Straits Lake. Across the street from the house was also a wooded area and the homes were very spread out, so the only neighbors on our side of the street were to the East. I don't remember thinking much about the move until the day we arrived. There was a dead cat in the driveway. I watched as one of the church volunteers, who helped us move, pick up the cat with a shovel and flung it into the woods.

I remember starting kindergarten and trying to make friends. I didn't really realize at the time that I was one of the only kids with a single mother, and that I was from one of the least expensive homes in the area. I remember trying to be friendly to the other kids, but I didn't react well when they would do something I didn't like. I developed very high morals from my mother's religious training. I was friendly and polite. I never stole, cursed or purposely broke any rules of the home or the school. However, when someone did something that seemed to be an attack on me, I felt that the person must be punished, and I was going to take this into my own hands to correct their wrongdoing.

By third grade, I was one of the bigger boys, and I continued this same pattern of behavior. If anyone crossed me, he should be taught a lesson.

Teachers would try to tell me to just walk away, but it didn't seem possible, so I ended up in many fights that year. I got into a fight during the last week of school in third grade, and the principal suspended me from attending the end of the year party on the last day of school. Of course, I thought my punishment was extremely unfair. None of the fights that I had gotten into were started by me. I was nice and kind to others. Why should I be punished? I was only trying to help out society by teaching these other boys a lesson.

I remember reading the letter from my teacher, typed up on an old typewriter. She listed the dates of my fights, which appeared to be every couple of weeks. Usually, these fights consisted of pushing, punching or pinning someone up against the wall until a teacher came to break us up. However, the last fight I got into that year was a little worse. I was carrying a baseball bat in from the playground, and some boy said to me that I couldn't play baseball if I tried. Now, since I truly believed I was going to be one of the greatest Detroit Tiger players ever, how could he disrespect me like this? I ran toward him swinging the baseball bat. Luckily, for him and me, he was able to run from me. I justified it in my mind that he deserved to be punished for this outrageous comment. It was very difficult for me to stay home that day when I knew my classmates were having fun at the last day of school party. What did they think of me?

Even though I was hurt by being suspended, what hurt me even worse was what a girl in my class, Rosemary, had said to me when I asked her which girls liked me. Rosemary responded, "Tom, none of girls like you because you get into too many fights." That hit me like a ton of bricks. I really wanted to be well liked and have the cute girls like me. How could I have the girls like me and still keep the mean boys in line? I thought a lot about this and thought maybe I *should* just walk away. I just couldn't come to grips with the solution to this dilemma.

Fourth grade started out somewhat better, because, well, how could it have been worse than third grade? I actually did walk away from many potential fights, but felt ashamed of myself for being so passive. The thoughts of feeling so disrespected would last for hours.

Academically, I could have been a good student through the fourth grade, but I rushed my work and made careless mistakes. For me, it was a competition to be the best. I wanted to be the first one done, and I wanted the highest grade on any assignment. Typically, I succeeded in being the first one done, but not in getting the highest grade. My thinking was that I was the best at everything and could show it by others seeing that I was the first one done with an assignment or test. It never crossed my mind to work in cooperation with the other top students. Maybe it was due to me being an only child. My report cards indicated that I made a lot of careless mistakes by rushing my work, but it didn't seem to matter to me.

Socially, I had a few casual friends with whom I played games and talked about *Batman*, *The Monkees* and *Laugh-in*, three popular television shows at the time. I only saw these friends at school and never asked them to come to my house. I didn't want them see how poor we were.

I had the album, "More of the Monkees" and I loved the song "She." I would sing it over and over. I thought that my voice sounded just like Micky Dolenz, one of the singers and the drummer for *The Monkees*. There is a line in the song, "she needs someone to walk on, so her feet don't touch the ground." I wasn't sure how to interpret that, but somehow I thought it was what I wanted in a girlfriend.

During the summers, my mother had me stay with her parents during the day and then would pick me up after she was done working. I enjoyed talking to Grandpa about sports. On weekends, I liked exploring the areas surrounding our home. I would ask my mother if I could go out, and I did almost every weekend. I would venture off into a path in the woods and then go down a hill that led to the lakefront homes on Upper Straights Lake. One of the homes was owned by Dr. Ray and Ruth Davis, who had met my mother and me at the West Bloomfield Baptist Church that we all attended. Dr. Davis was usually outside doing something in the yard. I rarely saw Mrs. Davis, because she stayed inside the house.

Soon after my last day suspension from third grade, Dr. Davis was out putting a new board in a picnic table, and I heard him say, "Tommy Boy."

I came over to where he was and said, "How are you, Dr. Davis?"

He responded, "I'm great as always, but please, call me Gramps."

I believe he was 60 years old at the time. I thought about telling him that I preferred being called Tom, but I decided to go along with "Tommy Boy" because he said it in such a pleasant way. I didn't think he was trying to disrespect me, but I did think of boys at school calling me names.

"Gramps, what are you working on?"

"I had to put a new board in this picnic table because it rotted over the winter." Then he asked me, "Do you know how to catch a bear?"

I looked at him, puzzled, and said, "No."

"You cut a hole in the ice and put a bunch of peas around it. When the bear comes to take a pea, you kick him in the ice hole," he said with a smile.

For a 9-year-old boy, hearing "take a pee" was very funny, and I giggled and laughed understanding the irony. However, it wasn't until years later that I also understood there was some irony in "ice hole" as well. Gramps often tried to make me laugh, so I always enjoyed talking to him when he was out.

Gramps was a family physician and had also worked as a professor at Michigan State University teaching others to be doctors. He worked one day a week in a family practice. He had the summers off from his position at the university. Gramps appeared to love his lake house and keeping up his property. I could see his front yard from the top of the hill. He kept the grass mowed and had many trees, shrubs and flowers. He had a long driveway, maybe 250 yards, which reached my street, Pontiac Trail. He had his own plow to remove snow in the winter.

Although Gramps was about ten years older than my grandparents, he seemed much younger. He was much thinner than Grandpa and much more active. He smiled a lot and usually couldn't wait to tell me something funny.

Gramps spent a lot of the time in his backyard. He had a huge deck off his back door with a lot of patio furniture. His backyard had a grassy area with trees and a sandy area that bordered Upper Straights Lake. He would bring in sand every year to keep up his own beach area. He also had a dock that protruded out into the lake, where he kept three rowboats. He also built a raft out of boards and steel drums, which had a surface area where each side was ten feet long that he would anchor it in the lake in about 15 feet of water. On the raft, he had built a ladder by welding pipes together. His entire property was very beautiful. I dreamed that this would be my home some day.

People could walk out into the water for about 30 to 50 feet (depending on your height) and then have to swim a short ways to the raft. Gramps enjoyed letting me swim there. I would only go as far as I could still touch bottom, but practiced swimming so that I could one day swim to the raft. Gramps also loved to have his adult children, their spouses, his grandchildren and other friends come to his house to swim and go for boat rides.

Just about every weekend day, I would look for Gramps. If he had heard about my school suspension from someone at church, he never said anything to me. I became more and more comfortable with him. One day, I told him that I had been suspended unfairly and told him about having to defend against people who had said mean things to me.

Gramps listened intently. Then Gramps asked me, "What are your goals for this year in fourth grade?"

"Goals? What do you mean?"

Gramps said, "What kind of grades do you want?"

"All A's."

He asked, "Did you get all A's this past year?"

I said that I got A's and B's and a C in handwriting.

Then he said, "So, if you want to get all A's this year, what are you going to do differently?"

I didn't have an immediate response to his question, so he asked me another question.

"What other goals do you have?"

I told him, "I want to have lots of friends and not get suspended. But if other people are mean to me, I won't reach that goal. I am always nice to others, but they still say mean things to me."

He asked me, "Do you expect everyone to be nice to you in the fourth grade?"

"Yes, I am nice, and they should also be nice. At church, we were taught to *do unto others as you would want them to do unto you*."

Gramps responded, "It seems to me like it is asking a lot of all the other fifth graders to always be nice to you. How many friends do you want?"

"I want everyone to be my friend."

"Tommy Boy, you are one of the finest young boys that I have ever met, but I don't know anyone whom everyone likes. I want you to meet your goals and be successful. I hope you will think about your goals and your plan to achieve them. I would be happy to help you with your plan."

"Would you fight the mean kids for me?"
"Tommy, one of my goals is to have peace in my life and not fight anyone except for an occasional spat with the wife when she tells me she doesn't want pizza on Friday nights."

I thought a lot about what Gramps had told me, and I did think a lot about my own goals. I vowed to never get suspended again. Also, I thought about what Rosemary had said. I was determined to do better in the fourth grade.

It turns out that I would go on to do somewhat better. I didn't get suspended. I got into less fights. I got more A's than B's. However, I still didn't have a lot of friends. I didn't know any of that then.

"Wild thing,
you make my heart sing,
you make everything,
groovy...I said wild thing"
— The Troggs (1966)

The First Practice

T he next day at school, after I had gotten the call telling me about the first practice, I saw my new coach's son, Stan, on the playground. I've interacted with Stan a few times since we go to the same school, but we had never been friends or done anything outside of school. I looked at Stan and said, "Hey."

Stan replied, "Hey, I hear you are on the team. Are you ready for a winning season?"

I responded, "I am. I'll be there on Monday."

Stan said, "See you then."

Stan would certainly be considered one of the most popular boys in the fourth grade. He was smart and a good student. He didn't get into much trouble. He was a very fast runner and was very good at most sports. Given that I am one of the better students too, it would seem like we would be good friends, but Stan lives about a mile from me and has a lot of boys to play with in his own neighborhood close to school.

I got home from school on Monday and tried to decide what to wear. I could wear blue jeans. I could wear cutoffs. Oh, I wish I knew what Stan was wearing. I decided on the cutoffs. Now, what shirt should I wear? Would a Detroit Tiger shirt look good or should I just wear a plain t-shirt? I decided on a plain blue t-shirt because I don't want to be the kid with the Tigers shirt or even worse, the kid with the *Monkees* or *Batman* shirt. I found my baseball socks, the ones with the two orange stripes at the top. Now, should I wear tennis shoes or baseball shoes? Baseball shoes would be better. I found my baseball shoes from last year. They were a tight fit, but they would have to work for the first practice, even though they were hurting my feet. I hoped I could get my mother to buy me some new ones.

For the last decision, do I wear a baseball hat? My hat from last year was a reminder of a poor season, so I didn't want to wear it. My other option was a Detroit Tiger cap with the old English D. I finally decided to go with no cap for the first practice. I stood and looked at myself in the mirror. I still wasn't sure this would make the best impression, but I decided it is better than any alternatives.

When my mother got home from work, I said hello to her, and then I grabbed my mitt and ball and went outside throwing the ball in the air. Later, I went in the house and got dressed as planned. My mother gave me a snack, and we headed over to Twin Beach Elementary for practice. I kept thinking that I wanted to do really well. It was a warm, cloudy day for the first practice. We arrived at the school. and we found my team at the closest field to the parking lot. I knew several of the boys, but there were some I didn't know.

One boy looked different from all the rest. He talked differently too. I remember from an *F Troop* episode that a Japanese warrior was a fierce martial arts fighter and this boy had eyes like that Samurai warrior.

He walked up to me and put his hand out to shake hands and said, "Hi, I'm Art."

I hesitated a little because it was unusual for boys at my school to shake hands. Secondly, I thought he might have tried to flip me on my back. I put out my hand and shook his hand. He had a very strong grip. He and one other boy were the only boys on the team as tall as I was. I responded to him, "Hi, I'm Tom."

I later learned that Art was born in Korea and had been adopted. He had only been in the United States for a few years. He went to a different elementary school than me with two other players on the team. The rest of the players on the team attended my elementary school.

Stan's father, whom I was told to call Coach, gathered all of us for a quick meeting. "Boys, we're going to have a lot of fun this year, but we are going to practice hard and play hard. All of you need to get along and respect each other. There won't be any arguing with each other, any umpires or me. What I say goes. If anyone needs to talk to an umpire, it will be me and me only. That goes for parents too. No arguing with umpires and no negative words should be said by parents about any of these fine young men. I expect to hear nothing but support, encouragement and praise when the players do well. None of you are Al Kaline or Denny McLain yet. You all have a lot to learn, so I hope you will all listen to me, try to get better, have some success and have fun. We will start by taking infield practice. I know you were all hoping for hitting, but we have to be able to get people out. Art and Jeff, both of you get a catcher's mitt and go to home plate. Joe, Will and Reggie, go to third. Stan and Mark go to short. Paul, Dave and Chuck take second. Bill and Tom take first. Now, let's practice!"

As soon as he said this, Stan, Joe and Will started running to their positions. I saw this and took off running to first. I wanted to establish myself as the starting first baseman. Bill took off too, but got there after me.

Coach yelled out, "Now, let's get one." He hit the ball down to Joe at third, who picked the ball up cleanly and threw a high throw to me at first. I reached up and caught it keeping my foot on the base. "Good play," Coach commented, "Now, Tom, after you make the play, get off the base and throw the ball to the catcher."

I did as Coach said and was thrilled that he knew my name. Coach then hit the ball to Stan at shortstop, who threw a little wide to me. I was able to keep my foot on the base and stretch my arm to catch the ball. After making the play, I got off the base and threw the ball to the catcher. I was starting to think I was pretty good at this. He then hit the ball to the second baseman. Paul was there, but threw the ball so low that the ball hit the ground before it got to me. Good first basemen are able to put their gloves in a position so that the ball hits the ground and the ball still gets into the glove. This is called catching the ball on the short hop. I tried to short hop it, but the ball bounced out of my glove. I quickly picked it up with my foot on the base.

Coach yelled, "Paul, get the throw up. Tom, you need to squeeze the glove."

Coach then hit one to me, and I was able to field it and run over to touch first. We kept this going for a while and kept rotating with the other players who were playing the same positions.

I made a short hop catch with a throw that hit in the dirt and could hear Coach saying, "Tom, great play!"

Bill rotated with me, but really struggled. He didn't have a first baseman's glove like I did and had a hard time moving to the base and making plays. Coach really didn't give him a lot of coaching after awhile. Bill was destined for the outfield.

Next, we took turns batting with Coach pitching. He was throwing fairly easy. He called each player when it was his turn to hit. All of the players got a chance to bat. He would tell each player, "Hold the bat back and swing evenly. We want line drives."

I'm not sure why, but I was the last hitter to hit. I'm hoping it was because he didn't want to put anyone else at first base. "Has everyone hit?" Coach yelled. I responded that I still hadn't hit.

Coach said, "Tom, get a helmet and get up there. Bill, take first."

I got my helmet on and grabbed a bat. I wasn't too worried about the Coach throwing at me. so I was thinking most pitches would be strikes. I hit a few balls that traveled high in the air.

Coach said, "Tom, those are going to be outs and no different than striking out. I need you to swing more level and hit some line drives."

It sounded like Coach had confidence in me. What a total turnaround from last season! It was as if he saw something in me and wanted to get the best out of me. At least this is what was going through my mind. I responded and tried to swing more level. I hit a ground ball to shortstop.

Coach said, "Tom, much better! You will get on base a lot more hitting the ball on the ground then in the air."

I finished up thinking I had done well batting. Gramps had talked to me about goals. and I decided that two of my goals were to be the starting first baseman and to bat third in the lineup.

The next day at school, I saw Stan at recess. "Tom, you looked good last night. You really impressed my dad. He was worried about having a good first baseman. He had thought about Will, but Will pitches and plays short and third when Joe or I pitch. You should come to the field behind Marty's house on Sunday afternoon and play with us."

"Thanks Stan! You looked really good too. I'd like to come to Marty's field. I'll check and see if I can make it."

I really wanted to be friends with Stan, and now it seemed like I had the opportunity. Could I be friends with him without getting angry at him about something? I was determined to try.

"See you at practice tomorrow," said Stan as he walked on.

The next practice went even better. I was playing a good first base and was hitting the ball well with Coach pitching to me. I guess most players on the team had taken what the coach had said to heart because there weren't a lot of negative comments, and I was enjoying playing. Stan came up to me after practice and asked me to come to his house on Sunday, and we would walk to Marty's baseball field. My mother was right there and she agreed. Stan was not only the coach's son, but he was our best hitter, fielder and pitcher. Stan seemed to have it all, and now I had the chance to be his friend. I did not want to do anything to mess this up.

On Friday, I was sitting in class, and someone passed me a note, which of course, was highly against the rules. The note said, "Penny likes you. Do you like her?" Penny had red hair and freckles. I'm not sure I found her to be the best looking girl in the class, but I liked the attention and wanted to see where it would lead, so I wrote on the note, "Yes" and handed it back. On its way back to Penny, Drew read the note. I always felt a little bad for Drew because I had thought his parents named him after they attended an art class. Later during the afternoon recess, Drew looked at me and sang the first line of "Tom and Penny sitting in a tree, K-I-S-S-I-N-G."

Oh, no! Why did I answer the note? My heart started to beat faster, and I replied to him, "I don't like her."

He responded that he saw what I wrote, and I said in denial, "I didn't write that."

I was still acting like my angry self when I heard any negative comments, but I didn't try to fight on impulse without thinking like I did in the third grade. Hurtful comments still bothered me a lot.

The Baseball Bat

"One is the loneliest number
that you'll ever do.
Two can be as bad as one.
It's the loneliest number
since the number one."
— Three Dog Night (1968)

Anger Control

After school on Friday, I asked Carol if I could take a walk to the lake, and she agreed as long as I didn't go in the water. I walked through the path in the woods and down the hill to Gramps' house to see if he was out.

As I walked back toward his backyard, I heard, "How's my Tommy?" I looked up and saw Gramps on the deck. He said, "It's Friday afternoon, and my work is done, and I was looking for someone to play horseshoes with me."

I smiled and agreed to play. Gramps had his own horseshoes and horseshoe pits, and he was really good. He threw a complete turn after his release of the shoe. I was still trying to throw horseshoes getting the shoe to flop one time in the air. If either of us were successful, the shoe would open up right as it got to the stake and have a chance of going around the stake. Of course, Gramps was much more successful than me. As we were playing, I told Gramps that I was doing better with my anger because I was walking away and wasn't fighting. But I still felt the same with my heart beating faster and feeling like I was out of control.

"Anger is the process of the heart beating faster, sweating and more rapid breathing. Whether you walk away or fight, you still feel anger. Walking away helps you avoid getting into trouble, but it doesn't help you avoid anger. That is why teachers tell you to walk away. They are more concerned about you not getting in trouble than helping you control your anger," said Gramps.

Gramps told me, "Anger is an important part of survival in the animal kingdom. If a rabbit is spotted by a wolf, the rabbit would need to get angry to be able to perform at its best to survive. So the brain sends signals to the body telling the rabbit to breathe faster, to get sweaty and for the heart to beat faster so the rabbit will be able to run its fastest and possibly survive its predator. With people, we have a big part of the brain behind our forehead, which is much more developed than animals. This part of the brain is called the frontal cortex and helps us think rationally and make logical decisions. When a person senses his or her life is in danger, the body kicks into survival mode, making the heart beat faster and causing the person to sweat more. This is when the ancient part of the brain takes over to help a person fight his or her best or run his or her fastest. All animals have this ancient part of the brain. The problem is that when this ancient part of the brain is in control, it is difficult to think rationally and make logical decisions."

By this time, Gramps is already leading in horseshoes, 17-4.

"So, anger is what I feel inside and not what I do?"

Gramps replied, "That's right, Tom. However, when we have this emotional reaction, it makes it very hard to control our behavior. That's four more points for me. Game over. Let's go sit on the picnic table."

"Okay, good game," I said.

"Tom, do you feel like hitting someone right now?" he said.

"No," I replied with a frown.

"However, you have felt like hitting people in the past and that is because the ancient part of your brain took over during anger and trumped your decision making part of the brain. You don't feel like hitting anyone now because you are thinking with your frontal cortex."

"Gramps, that makes sense to me, but why do I get angry when my life is not in danger?"

"Tom, that is because you actually perceive the situation as dangerous."

"No, I don't think it is dangerous when someone says something mean," I replied.

"It's good to hear you say that because when you think to yourself that what someone said is awful or you think that they should not have said it or that you can't stand what has just been said, your brain interprets these thoughts as dangerous," said Gramps.

"I can't really control my thinking. It's just how I feel," I said.

"Tom, if I was to give you $1,000 if you didn't get angry for 10 minutes, could you do it?"

"You bet I could."

"Wait a minute, it's not that simple. I would bring one of your classmates in for this exercise, and for 10 minutes they would call you names and say negative things about you. Could you do it?"

I had to think about this one. "Hmmm, I guess if I knew it was all in fun, and I would get a $1000, I could do it."

"No, this would not be in fun. This would be very real and very hurtful. However, if you could do it, you would get the money. Now if it were me, people could say anything for ten minutes, and I would make sure I got the money," he said.

"How would you do it?"

"For every hurtful thing that was said, I would focus on my goal of receiving the money. You may not believe this yet, but it is not what is said that makes people angry, it's a person's thoughts about what is said. I bet you know some boys and girls who don't seem to get angry when the same thing happens to them that happened to you," Gramps said.

"I do. I do. So, they are thinking different than me?"

"Yes, yes, yes, they are!" Gramps exclaimed.

"Gramps, I'm willing to change my thoughts. How do I do it?" I asked.

"Tom, it's not that easy. You can't go from getting angry one day to not getting angry the next. You have formed a habit—a bad habit. Here is what I want you to do. If you are truly in danger, I want you to get angry. However, if your life is not being threatened, I want you simply to say, 'my life is not being threatened, so this is not awful. I can stand it because I have stood this before. Just because I am a nice person, I cannot expect other people to think and act like me. This other person is just being him or herself.' It will take awhile, but if you really think this way, you will not be angry in time."

"I will try to think these thoughts, but what should I say to someone who says something rude?"

Gramps replied, "There is no easy answer, but let's do this. Tell me what happened at school, and we will see if there was another way to handle it."

I told Gramps about the note and Drew's reaction.

Gramps then asked me, "How do you think that Drew should have reacted seeing the note?"

"He shouldn't have sung the song with my name in it."

"I understand." said Gramps, "So a fourth grade boy should just think about how funny it is and not say anything?"

I thought about it for a minute and said, "He should show respect for me."

"Tom, every time you use the word *should*, you have expectations of how someone will act, and it will usually lead to anger," he said, "Wouldn't you expect Drew to be himself?"

"I guess so."

"Was the situation awful?" Gramps asked.

"Yes," I said firmly.

"Tom, let's establish this. If someone was trying to kill you by beating you with a baseball bat, would that be awful?"

"Yes," I said firmly again.

"Okay, which is worse? You have to choose. Someone singing a song about you or someone trying to kill you by beating you over the head with a baseball bat?"

I thought about it and said, "They would both be bad, but I guess that being hit over the head with a baseball bat would be worse."

"Tom, getting hit over the head with a baseball bat is much worse. In fact, it's awful and you wouldn't be able to stand it. However, you would be able to stand having a song sung about you because you just proved you could stand it this. Having a song sung about you is something you don't like, but it isn't awful, because you will live to see another day. It would help you if you tolerated things you don't like and got angry at things you can't stand. Does that make sense?"

"Yes, Gramps, it does make sense. So what should I have done while he was singing the song about me?"

Gramps responded, "What you did was use denial. You denied something for which there was clear evidence. Drew had seen the note. Telling him you didn't write it was a lie. Children learn denial at a young age to avoid punishment, but it doesn't work well at your age."

"So, if I don't deny, do I say I did it?"

"You don't have to admit it or deny it," Gramps replied, "Assuming you were able to think that he was acting like himself, that it wasn't awful and that you could stand it, you might have responded back in a calm manner. Humor is sometimes that best approach. How about saying, 'Drew, at least I have a girl that likes me.' You could then laugh and walk away."

"Gramps, that sounds good, but I have been getting angry and lashing out at people my whole life."

Gramps replied with a smile, "I'm betting you are going to live a long life, so much of your life is in front of you. You have gotten pretty good at throwing and catching a baseball. How long did it take you to be so good at that?"

"I worked on it every day for hours."

"Yes you did, and if you want to get good at anger control and good communication, you will have to work on it daily as well. For now, keep walking away, but come talk to me about what was said that caused you to walk away, and we will come up with a better response together, okay?"

"Okay, Gramps. Thank you. I'll try it. I better be getting home.

The Baseball Bat

"It's time we stop.
Children, what's that sound?
Everybody look what's going down."
— Buffalo Springfield (1966)

Neighborhood Game

On Saturday mornings, I would usually watch cartoons. If I got up early enough, I could catch *Go Go Gophers*. Then there would be some animates action shows like *Batman, Superman* and *Underdog.* I would then switch to the music-oriented shows, *Archie* or *Banana Splits,* as I would enjoy singing along with the lyrics and fill in the beats by singing word bump. "Oh, sugar, bump, bump, bump, bump, bump, bump/Oh honey, honey, bump, bump, bump, bump, bump, bump."

My mother would then take me to the laundromat and grocery store. As you can imagine, the laundromat wasn't that exciting, except for the time that a lady started bleeding by the wringer washer, and I thought she had put her hand through the wringer. As it turns out, she was just bleeding from scratched mosquito bites. My mother would give me a dollar for allowance, and I would usually spend it on baseball cards, because I liked the collecting aspect and reading the player statistics. When I would have extra money, I bought old coins, thinking they would be worth a lot of money some day. I would have never guessed that the coins never appreciated, but the baseball cards became worth some money. The grocery store was more exciting because I got to pick the cereal that I wanted—a cereal that usually had something free inside. Somehow, I valued the prize more than the taste of the cereal.

On Sunday, I was excited to go over to Stan's, but was very anxious about going to play baseball at Marty's field. My mother drove me to Stan's house, and I told her that I would walk home after playing baseball. I got to Stan's house and was amazed that it was a two-story home with a two-car garage. I dreamed that I would have a home like this someday. The house was huge by my standards, but it was probably just a middle class home. Stan invited me in, and we went to his room. I asked Stan if he collected baseball cards, and he pulled out his box to show me. He had some players I didn't have, and I had some he didn't have. I asked him if I could come back some day and trade with him and he agreed. He then showed me some of his toys. He had Rockem Sockem Robots. I had seen the advertisements on television about this game, but had never seen it in real life. We played and had fun, and then we walked to the field.

Marty's backyard was the size of a baseball field. I could tell why it was the best place to play. It was bordered by trees, so no houses could really be hit by baseballs. The only problem was that it wasn't as flat as most fields where games were played, so sometimes we had some interesting bounces.

Stan and I were actually two of the younger boys, but Joe was there too. Marty was a fourth grader, but he was a year older. He must have flunked a grade, but I never asked him. Most of the other boys played in the Bronco League for 11 and 12-year-olds. Since I was 10-years-old, I played in the Mustang League. Stan was telling me on the way over that they played Bronco League rules, which meant you could lead off and steal bases. In the Mustang League, we had to wait until the ball crossed the plate to steal.

As we arrived, everyone knew each other. Stan told me who some the guys were whom I didn't know, but they didn't really introduce themselves to me. We played catch for a while, and then one of the guys said that we needed to pick teams. I kept waiting for someone to pick me, but I ended up being the last one picked. I was humiliated. At least I got on the same team with Stan. There was no adult supervision. The older boys just took control. Our team took the field first. I ran out to first base, but a guy older and taller than me was already there.

He said, "What's your name?" and I told him and he said, "Tom, why don't you take right field?"

I trotted out to right field, but was not very happy about it.

I made it through the first inning with nothing coming my way. I was really worried that I wouldn't be able to handle the ball if it came to me, and I would look foolish. I didn't get to bat in the first inning either. Since I was the last pick, I was the last hitter. In the second inning, a ground ball got between first and second, and I was able to field it and throw it back to the infielders. I was very nervous, but I was happy that I made the play.

In the bottom of the second inning, I got up to bat. Wow, this guy really threw hard. I was so worried the ball would hit me. I only swung once after taking two strikes and struck out. I got up for the second time and struck out again too.

In the next inning, someone actually hit a fly ball to right field, and it scared me, but I ran under it, stuck my first baseman's glove out and somehow got it to stick in my glove. I heard a few guys say "good catch" as I threw the ball in to the second baseman. The game broke up, and I said good-bye to Stan and walked home. I felt I had failed to show everybody how good I was. I felt embarrassed by my performance. Maybe everyone was still talking about how bad I was.

After getting home and eating dinner, I walked down the hill and found Gramps sitting on a picnic table near the sandy area, looking out at the lake.

As I approached, Gramps asked, "What did the painter say to wall?"

I thought and said, "I don't know."

"One more crack like that and I'll plaster you," he replied with a smile.

I laughed and laughed.

He said, "I like that one. It is also funny because it's hard to believe that if someone just says something, that someone else would plaster them."

The word plaster back then was slang for beating someone in a fight.

"Gramps, when you say it like that, it does sound funny," I said, "Why are you out here?"

"I love to look at the lake this time of day. It's so peaceful. The lake looks like a sheet of glass.

Nothing is more calming," he said, "How was your day?"

"It was a terrible day."

"Oh, no!" Gramps replied, "Someone tried to hit you with a baseball bat? How did you escape?"

"Okay, okay, it wasn't awful, but it felt very bad. I was picked last in the neighborhood game and struck out both times up," I said sadly.

"Well, it sounds like we better start from the beginning, so I can hear about your whole day."

I went on to tell him about the day.

"So, you had a good time with a new friend you wanted to be friends with, you got to go to his house and see his collections and his games, you got to play in the neighborhood game for the first time, the guys were generally nice to you and didn't say anything negatively and you made a catch in the outfield. This was a terrible day?"

"I guess there were some good points and some bad points to the day."

Gramps replied, "Well, if you have started a friendship with Stan, it sounds like one of the best days you've had in awhile. Where did you expect to get picked being the only one who hadn't played in the neighborhood game before? How did you expect to bat having never faced these older boys' pitching before?"

"Gramps, you're right as always. I guess I should have expected to be picked last, and I should have expected to struggle against their pitching since I had never practiced against it before."

"So, Tommy Boy, how was your day?" he asked with a smile.

I just smiled and laughed a little. "Gramps, why do I do this to myself?"

"People generally focus on the negative. It's part of survival. Animals focus on where the predators are and not what good has happened to them. However, people have the ability to focus on the positive aspects of their lives, and those who choose to do that tend to be happier," Gramps said again, with a smile, "Now how can any day be anything but good when the water is this calm?"

"Gramps, thank you."

I sat and stared out at the peaceful lake and started feeling good about the day: how lucky I was to have Stan becoming my friend and how *really* lucky I was to have Gramps in my life.

"Come on Baby, light my fire.
Come on Baby, light my fire.
Trying to set the night on fire."
— *The Doors (1967)*

First Game

T he next morning, my mother called my name and said that it was time to get up and go to school. I could hear her say, "I'm not calling you again." I looked at the clock and jumped out of bed. We didn't have a shower, so each morning I took a "bird bath," which consisted of washing with a washcloth and washing my hair by putting my head upside down in the sink. One thing I had noticed about Stan's house was that he had a shower. I dreamt that one day when I was famous, I would have a shower. I got dressed and had some time for cereal. This week, I had chosen Honey Comb to get my free prize. The prize was a *Rocket Jet*, which looked cool in the commercial, but it turned out to be just a cheap plastic airplane with a rubber band. Honey Comb was not my favorite, but I knew I had to eat it since I had asked for it. My mother would not be happy throwing any food out.

As I walked out the door, I could hear the famous call by the neighbor children, "the bu-us," which was stretched out to 5 seconds and three syllables. I ran to my side of the road as the bus arrived. The driver turned on the stoplights, and I was able to cross the street to·get on the bus with the traffic stopped. I grabbed a seat by myself, which was my normal practice.

A few bus stops later, a boy got on the bus and plopped down next to me, bumping me as he sat down. I thought about what Gramps had told me. This is not a dangerous situation. He is not hitting me with a baseball bat. Then I had a humorous thought that he put his life in danger bumping me. I laughed a little. Where should he have sat? He should sit in an open seat. I decided I could stand the situation and went on daydreaming about baseball.

When I walked into the classroom, I saw Penny. Should I say something to her? What should I say? What would others say if they saw me talking to her? She looked over, and I quickly turned away and took my seat. I made it through the day without talking to her at all.

The most interesting thing about the day was one boy in my class apparently said a curse word because he had to have a bar a soap in his mouth for about ten minutes. I'm glad I never had a bar of soap in my mouth. That seemed really bad to me. I made it through the rest of the day without anyone saying anything negatively toward me. Sadly, I guess I had trained people to somewhat avoid me.

When I got home, I headed down to the lake to see if Gramps was out. I didn't see him, but he had allowed me to come down and sit where I chose. My choices were the picnic table, the dock or a log that borders the sandy beach area and the grass. I chose to sit on the top of the picnic table with my feet on the seat.

I looked out at the lake as I thought about my day and the upcoming weeks. Can I really use what Gramps said about anger? Did I really do it today? What should I do about Penny? Should I try to talk to her? I have the first game coming up this Saturday. Am I ready to be the star?

—◆—

We had two more baseball practices on Tuesday and Thursday of that week. These were really our last two practices because starting Saturday, we had games every Tuesday, Thursday and Saturday for 15 games with one open Tuesday for a makeup game if we had a rainout.

On Tuesday, Art and I arrived early to practice, so we talked a little about school. I wanted to ask him what it was like looking different than the other boys, but I didn't know if that was appropriate to say. I found out that he liked to have fun, play games and collect trading cards like me. After we had talked, I was much more comfortable with him the rest of the season.

On Thursday, Coach handed out our uniforms and hats. I say uniforms because that is what they were to me, but the uniforms consisted of just a red T-shirt with Lakes Athletic Association on the front and a number, and our sponsors', Penny Lake Grocery, advertising on the back. He started with the smaller boys. There were six 9-year-olds on the team and six 10-year-olds. He pulled out the first uniform, which had a number one on it and gave it to Mark, a 9-year-old. He then gave uniforms 2, 3 and 4 to Chuck, Reggie and Jeff, all 9-year-olds, respectively. I could see that the smaller kids were getting the low numbers. I wondered if I would get number 25 and have the same number as the first baseman of the Detroit Tigers, Norm Cash.

Coach continued handing out shirts. The next five uniforms went to the other 10-year-olds. Stan got number 5, Jim Northrup's number. Art got number 6, Al Kaline's number. Paul, Joe and Will got numbers 7, 8 and 9, respectively. I was prepared for number 10, but Dave, a 9-year-old, got number 10. He then called me for number 11. If the choices were 1 to 12, then I did pretty well because I got the number of Detroit Tiger all-star catcher, Bill Freehan. I was happy with the number. Bill, the other guy who tried to play first base, got uniform 12. Coach then handed out the hats with me getting the largest size. I put my hat on and wore it proudly. It was a red cap with a white letter C for the Cardinals.

Coach then called us in to speak to us. "We have our first game on Saturday. Go to bed early so you will be well rested. Everyone will play, but we can only start 9 players. Art, you will lead off and catch. Stan, you will bat second and play short."

I was getting scared. I really wanted to bat third and play first base.

I then heard the Coach continue, "Joe, you will bat third and pitch. Will, you will bat fourth and play third."

I was getting upset. I was saying to myself, "Please fifth."

"Paul, you will bat fifth and play second. Tom, you will bat sixth and play first base. "

I was relieved that I was starting, but not happy about my place in the order.

"Dave, you will play left and bat seventh. Bill, you play right and bat eighth, and Mark, you'll play center and bat ninth. Okay, I'll see everyone Saturday at 8:30 to warm up for the 9:00 game."

I didn't say anything. I was the tallest boy on the team, and I was batting last among the 10-year-olds.

Stan came up to me and said, "I told my dad to give you a Detroit Tigers' number. Look, we're Northrup and Freehan. We're going to play like them. Norm Cash usually bats sixth in the Detroit Tigers' order."

I tried to hide my disappointment. "Stan, this is exciting! We are going to have a great year. See you Saturday."

I got in the car and didn't say anything to my mother.

My mother asked, "Are you excited about your uniform?"

"Mom, I like my uniform, but coach is batting me last."

"Tom, I thought you were sixth?"

"I am last among the 10-year-olds. I'm going to show Coach that he made a mistake with the batting order," I said angrily.

I was not using my anger techniques that Gramps had taught me. I could only think about batting sixth, or as I called it, last, in the order. I calmed down a little when I thought about what Stan had said about Norm Cash batting sixth. I didn't have a choice. This was where I would bat, and I vowed to do my very best to play well.

Saturday morning came and I couldn't wait to get to the field. There was a game field set up in back of Shepherd of the Lakes Lutheran Church. I put my t-shirt and hat on proudly. Stan and I were two of the first to get to the field, so we started playing catch.

We were the away team, so we got to bat first. The Dodgers' pitcher was struggling to get the ball over the plate. He walked Art on four pitches. Art stole second on the first pitch. Art and Stan were the two fastest runners on the team. Stan got up and walked too. Joe swung at a couple bad pitches and struck out. If only I had been in that third spot, I thought. Will was next up and hit a ground ball past third base for a double. Art scored and Stan went to third. Will then stole second on the first pitch. Paul hit a ground ball to the second baseman, who threw him out, but Stan scored and Will went to third.

It was my turn, and I stepped in wanting to hit, even though I could hear Coach saying, "Pick a good pitch."

The first pitch looked good enough to me, and I hit a ground ball toward short. I took off running as fast as I could. The shortstop bobbled it a little and then threw to first base a little late. I had beaten it out. Yes! I will record this as an infield hit, I thought. Since I keep my own stats, I am my own official scorer, so it was ruled a base hit. I also get an RBI (run batted in) because Will scored. I am hitting 1.000. On the first pitch, I tried to steal. Luckily, I slid in before the second baseman could tag me. I would be able to add a stolen base to my stat sheet. I didn't end up scoring, but we led 3-0.

I got up to bat three more times in the game. The next time up, I grounded to the pitcher for a putout at first base. My third time up there was a runner on second, and I hit a ground ball between short and third. The shortstop got his glove on it, but deflected it out in back of third. By the time the left fielder got it, I was at second for my first double and another RBI. Again, if it doesn't sound like a solid double, I was my own official scorer, and I erred on the side of my favor. I ended up scoring this time after an error by the other team on Dave's ground ball.

The last time up that day, the relief pitcher missed badly on the first two pitches, and I could hear Coach yelling, "Tom, good eye."

I ended up walking and getting another stolen base. Stan, who had come on to pitch in the fourth inning, saved the game by striking out the last three batters, and we won the game 10-5. I got home and entered my stats on a piece of notebook paper. I also included the five putouts I made at first base.

Then I had to do what I bet none of the Detroit Tigers had to do. I had to go to the laundromat and grocery store with my mother. When I got home, I wanted to go to the lake to look for Gramps. My mother told me that I couldn't be too long, because we were going to Grandma and Grandpa Mochina's house later. I went down and saw Gramps cleaning out one of his rowboats. I had to change my T-shirt so my mother could wash it, but I still had my hat on.

"Tommy Boy! How's Tommy Boy?" I could hear him say.

For some reason, hearing Gramps call me Tommy Boy always put a smile on my face, no matter what my mood was.

"Gramps, I had my first game today. Two for three and a walk, two RBIs, two stolen bases, a run scored and 5 putouts at first," I said proudly.

Gramps replied, "I think the Detroit Tigers could use you. Great game!"

Gramps then asked me, "Did you hear the joke about the roof?"

"No," I replied, wondering what he would say.

Gramps said, "Oh, I can't tell you...because it's over your head."

I laughed and laughed. It was always fun to be around Gramps. Then he said, "So how's your love life? Are you able to fight away all of the girls who want you to be their boyfriend?"

I said with a smile, "Yes, it is tough, but I am trying to keep them away. I told you that I got a note that a girl liked me last Friday."

Gramps smiled and said, "Oh, did you kiss her yet?"

I blushed, "No, I haven't even talked to her."

Gramps smiled again, "Well, what you are waiting for? I would have taken her out in the rowboat by now and kissed her."

I just laughed and said, "I thought about talking to her, but I felt nervous about what to say."

Gramps replied, "Hi, I'm Tom Mochina, the best looking, smartest, most athletic guy in the school, and I'm going to let you be my girlfriend for awhile until I find someone better."

We both just laughed. I knew I wouldn't say that, but I think Gramps was trying to tell me to be more confident.

—◆—

Later that night, I went to my grandparents' house. They lived in Ferndale, which I considered to be in the city. It had sidewalks. All of the houses were close together and all looked alike. Everyone there had very small yards. I got an uneasy feeling being outside there. My grandparents had a house that would be considered a Cape Cod style home, with two small bedrooms downstairs and one bedroom upstairs with a sloped ceiling. They had one bathroom, but it was bigger than ours and had a shower. They had a one-car detached garage. We had no garage. Stan had a 2-car-garage. Gramps had a two car-garage and a boathouse. I started to believe that there was a special status in how big of a garage one had.

I enjoyed talking to my grandfather because he listened to every Detroit Tigers' game on the radio, except for the occasional weekend televised game that he got to watch.

As I walked in, Grandpa said, "I heard you had a good game today."

"Yes, we won," as I continued to tell him my entire stat line, "How did the Tigers do?"

Grandpa said, "Great. The Tigers beat the Yankees 7-0 and now have 9 wins with only 3 losses. McAuliffe and Northrup hit homeruns and *there has never been any like old near-sighted Denny*. Mickey Mantle couldn't touch him today."

Grandpa was referring to the radio song about Denny McLain, who pitched wearing glasses. Mickey Mantle was one of the most famous players of the day, and as it turned out, it was his final season in the big leagues. It was special that McLain held one of the greatest hitters ever, hitless.

Then, there was a knock at the door and a man came in and introduced himself as Mr. Pete. His hair looked thin and greasy. He appeared to be dressed in work clothes. He had a strange laugh as he spoke.

My mother said, "Tom, we are going out for a little while. I'll be back later."

I didn't say much. I didn't like the looks of this guy. There was no way he was going to be my father.

Take a load off Annie.
Take a load for free.
Take a load off Annie.
And you put the load right on me.
— *The Band (1968)*

The Machine

On Monday at school, I saw Penny as we were waiting for school to start. She was by herself, so I walked up and said, "Hi."

"Hi, Tom, how are you?"

I was wearing my baseball hat, still proud from the win, and I said, "I'm good. We won our first baseball game. I had two hits, two RBIs and two stolen bases." I guess I would gladly tell anyone willing to listen about the game, even though it probably didn't mean much to her. Last year, I never told anyone about any of the games.

She said, "Oh that's nice. Tom, I think you're cute."

I was speechless. All I could say was, "Well, have a good day," and went to my seat.

I got to my seat and my heart was pounding. How did the reply for my impressive stats end up with me being cute? Maybe I should have said something back to her. I remembered the popular religious TV commercial that I repeated often, "That old man could have said a lot of things, but what he did say was..." Maybe I should have told her that she was cute. Maybe at least I should have said thank you. I handled this poorly. My thought was that I needed wisdom from Gramps. I made it through the day, but I really felt uncomfortable.

—◆—

On Tuesday, we had our second game of the season; this time was against the Indians. Joe and Stan shared the pitching duties again, but we lost 6-4. I struck out, popped out and hit a ground ball up the middle for a base hit to drop my average to .500. In the first inning, Will threw a ball in the dirt to me, and I was able to short-hop the ball into my glove and get the guy out at first.

I heard one parent say, "That guy is a machine at first. He can scoop anything."

In the third inning, I also caught one on the short hop. I had practiced it with the pitch back net, and I knew I just had to get the big first baseman glove in the right position and the glove would do the rest. It looked much more impressive than it actually was.

"The Machine! The Machine!" I heard another parent say.

At first, I thought they were making fun of my last name. I knew I had an unusual last name. I wasn't sure if the parents were disrespecting me, making fun of my last name or they appreciated my play at first.

After the game was over, a couple of parents said to me, "Tom, good game. You are 'The Machine' at first because you make all the plays."

I just said, "Thank you," but I didn't smile. Why should I? We had just lost, and we were not going undefeated this year.

I thought a lot about being called The Machine. Stan was called "The Man" because of

Stan Musial's nickname. Maybe that is why we were the Cardinals, because of Stan "The Man" Musial. "The Man" sounded a lot better than "The Machine." I wasn't a machine like a candy dispenser. I found it odd, but I eventually accepted it and was proud to have a nickname like some of the major league players.

Stan came up to me after the game and said, "Hey, we didn't get the win today, but you did look good at first base."

"Stan, I really appreciate it. I'm disappointed. I wanted to go undefeated. You pitched great."

"Thanks, Tom. See you at the next game. We're a good team. We'll bounce back."

We finished out the week winning Thursday, but losing on Saturday. Saturday was the first game of the season that I did not get a hit. Besides not getting a hit, there was one really strange play. Stan was playing shortstop and he made a good throw to me. I caught the ball and then came off the base to throw the ball around the horn, and I heard the umpire yell, "Safe."

I turned and stared at him.

The umpire said, "You pulled your foot off the base before you caught it."

I was sure he was wrong. After that inning, I came in and asked the Coach about it. He told me that it looked to him like I was on the base, but apparently this umpire didn't like how quickly I got off the base.

Coach told me, "Perception is a big part of baseball, just like it is in life. You would do better if you kept your foot on the base just a little bit longer, so there could be no doubt in the umpire's mind."

I was still mad at the umpire when I got up to the plate, and unfortunately, was thinking more about him than I was about hitting, and I tapped the ball to the first baseman for an easy out.

After the Saturday trips to do the laundry and grocery shopping, I asked my mother if I could go to the lake. As I went down the hill, I saw Gramps out mowing his lawn. Gramps shut the mower off and said, "Hey Tom, I've got some cushions that serve as life preservers in one of the row boats and it's pulled up on shore. Do you want to take the boat out for awhile?"

"Wow, that would be great."

I hustled down to the boat and pushed it out as I jumped in. I started rowing like I had seen Gramps and others do. I didn't go too far out, but I got to see from the lake what the houses looked like. I got to see people's docks and boats. I had fun rowing. I saw people out swimming and playing. I couldn't help but think about what Gramps had said about kissing a girl in the boat. I would kiss a girl in the boat someday. I knew I would. As I brought the boat back in, Gramps was just about finished mowing.

"Wow, Gramps, thank you so much. That was so much fun!" I exclaimed.

"Anytime, just let me know."

I hung up the boat cushions in the boathouse and Gramps asked me, "Did you get a kiss from that girl at school yet?"

"Gramps, come on. In school? Hey, I did talk to her. I walked up and said hi."

"What did she say?"

"She told me she thought I was cute."

"Tom, that meant she wanted to kiss you," Gramps said with a smile.

"Alright, maybe I will next time," not letting on that I was terrified of even talking to her.

"How's baseball?" asked Gramps.

"We're at two wins and two losses. The umpire made a bad call on me today, but the coach taught me to adjust to give the umpire the right perception. My mother is dating some jerk, Mr. Pete. I'm not happy about that. He really looks weird."

"Tom, it's tough on your mother to be raising you alone. It's good for her to date sometimes."

"I know, but I still don't like him."

"Hey, Tom, I've got one for you. Why is a dog with a broken leg like adding 6 plus 7?" Gramps asked me, waiting for my answer, "You put down the three and carry the one."

"Gramps, thanks again for letting me take the boat out," I said as I walked away, still laughing at the joke.

On Sunday, I had fun singing along with the transistor radio. I decided I was going to be both a rock and roll singer and a professional baseball player. I had used my allowance to buy a Mad Magazine. They had changed the words to several familiar tunes. Instead of "Hello Dolly," using the same tune, they had changed it to "Hello deli, this is Joe, deli. Would you please send up some nice corned beef on rye?" They had changed "Downtown" to "Ground Round." My favorite was changing to the words to "I'm Looking Over a Four Leaf Clover" to a song about Christopher Columbus, which started out, "I had a notion to cross the ocean that I'd never crossed before. I thought for certain that Asia I'd reach. Now, something tells me, I've hit the wrong beach." I sang that song over and over, thinking it was so funny.

Music gave me so much pleasure, and the combination of music and humor was what I enjoyed the most. Many of the new songs back then were about love. At only ten years old, I didn't quite understand love, but I was fascinated by romantic relationships.

Sunday was a musical day. My mother heard me and wanted sing a song for me from when she was younger. Her song made me laugh and laugh. I remember it started out, "There once was a farmer who had a young miss. In the back of the barn where he gave her a...lecture on horses and chickens and eggs."

I really enjoyed singing with my mother. I could tell she was happy when she sang. She mainly spent her time working, doing chores around the house or talking on the telephone. Sometimes she would sing with the choir at church. It was fun to watch her at church since most of the time she was taking me to baseball games and watching me. She had some friends from the church choir, but most of her friends were Hungarian immigrants from the city. I once tried to ask her about when we moved out to our house away from the city, but I could see tears in her eyes, so I never asked again. She did spend a lot of time talking to her friends and family on the telephone. I felt at home, and I never wanted to move back to the city.

I thought about what Gramps had said about my mother dating. I understood that my mother wanted adult companionship, but I had a lot of fears of how my life might change with a man in her life. Maybe she would want to move back to the city. Maybe I wouldn't be allowed to be in activities.

The Baseball Bat

Flipping Out

O n Monday, I arrived at school to find that the teacher had changed the seating chart. I was moved to the second row in the middle. The desks in this classroom were the individual seats with the writing board attached. The desk was made of wood and metal with a smooth writing surface. The writing area could be lifted to store books and school supplies underneath. What bothered me about the new seating arrangement was this boy sitting behind me, Don, who squirmed in his seat a lot. He would hit the back of my chair with his feet from time to time. One time, he hit my seat a little harder than he had previously, and I turned and stared at him for about 5 seconds. He just seemed to smile and kept squirming. He was clueless that I was trying to intimidate him with my size and mean look in my attempt to get him to stop.

By Wednesday of that week, I was getting really annoyed from him putting his feet on my seat. It reminded me of a time over the Christmas holiday break when my mother took me to a *walk-in* theatre for the first time, and the guy behind me kicked my seat. Before this, I had only been to The Commerce Drive-In to see movies. The *walk-in* concept, now known as movie theaters, was new to me. After experiencing both walk-ins and drive-ins, I decided I liked drive-ins better to avoid people bothering me.

My heart was beating faster, and I knew that I was getting angry. Don kicked the seat again. I stood up and lifted up so hard on his writing area of his desk that the entire desk toppled backward, so that Don had landed on his back. The teacher and the rest of the class stared in surprise. I sat back down in my seat hoping that the class would just continue, but teacher asked to see both Don and me in the hall.

The teacher asked, "Tom, why did you do that?"

"I think Don got what he deserved. Since you changed the seating arrangement, he has been kicking my chair all week. I turned around several times and glared at him, but he wouldn't stop. Do you have a better solution?"

"Yes, I do, Tom," she said, "Come and talk to me before you get to the point where you disrupt the entire class. Don, what do you have to say for yourself?"

Don replied, "I never kicked his chair. I don't know what he is talking about."

"Liar!" I snapped.

"Boys, I'm going to put together a new seating chart after lunch," she said, "Now, let's all go in and take your seats, so I can finish the lesson."

We returned to the classroom and made it through the lesson without incident. After lunch, we had a new seating chart. I sat in my new desk, satisfied that my seat would not be touched. However, people avoided talking to me that day. My goals were to not get angry and to have lots of friends. I did get angry, and I don't believe I did a lot to help people get in line to be my friend. At least school would be out for the summer in a month, so I wouldn't have to face the people in this class for a few months. I was hoping Gramps would be out, so I could talk to him about what happened at school. I hoped he wouldn't be disappointed in me. After school, I went down the hill and sat on Gramps' picnic table, but I never saw Gramps. Eventually, I went back up and waited for my mother to get home.

Our game on Tuesday was rained out, but we did have a game on Thursday. We played the Dodgers again, and I was able to get two more hits and steal two more bases. We won the game and now had a record of three wins and two losses. I made every play at first base except for one throw that was over my head and out of reach. Some parents still made comments about me being "The Machine" when I would make a play at first. I was still batting sixth in the lineup. Coach changed around the seventh through ninth spots a little, but never altered the first six spots. Art seemed to walk about half the time. Maybe the pitchers were afraid of him. After he would walk, he had such good speed that he usually scored. Of course, Stan hit behind him, and he must have been hitting about .800. The desk-flipping incident was not brought up at any point during the game, but I knew that many of my teammates had heard about it.

—✦—

On Friday after school, I went down to the lake and saw Gramps this time.

"Tommy Boy, the star first baseman, how are you?"

I had not told Gramps about being called "The Machine" because I didn't want him calling me that.

"Gramps, remember when you taught me about having goals and controlling my anger?"

"Well, of course, how has that been going?"

"I have done well. I have been able to control my anger in many situations where previously I would have lost control. I am really trying to focus on my goals and stand some situations that I don't like, but...," I hesitated, "I did have a problem this week."

"Tom, come sit on the picnic table and tell me about it."

Gramps had a way of making me feel comfortable, no matter what I had to say. We both sat on the top of the picnic table. I told him the story of what had happened.

"There is an important rule about anger management that I haven't told you. No one is perfect, and everyone makes mistakes. Do you believe that?"

"You don't ever seem to make any mistakes," I said.

Gramps laughed and said, "I have made many more mistakes than you. In my sixty years, I have learned a lot from my mistakes and try not to make them again, but every once in awhile, I still do. Wednesday was my fifth wedding anniversary, and I completely forgot about it. When I woke up,

Mrs. Davis had a present for me. She was very upset with me for forgetting our anniversary, so I had to quickly call the Rooster Tail restaurant down on the Detroit River to make reservations. We went there on Wednesday, so I was able to do some damage control, but I still made a mistake."

"Gramps, wow, I can hardly believe you forgot your anniversary. You have only been married 5 years? How can that be? You have adult children."

"Tom, I was married 13 years to my first wife, less than 3 years to my second wife and now five years to the third and hopefully last wife. Yes, I made many mistakes along the way, or I would have been married 37 years to the first wife. So, when you make a mistake, you cannot beat yourself up. You need to learn from your mistakes and move on. Sometimes you need to do what I had to do on Wednesday. Put your tail between your legs and beg for forgiveness."

I laughed when he said this. I also realized why he wasn't home when I came down on Wednesday.

"So, will the flipping of the desk episode haunt you forever? I bet it will be long forgotten by the start of fifth grade. You made a mistake. No big deal. Let's laugh it off and learn from it. Now, how should you have handled it instead?"

My response was the typical, "I guess I should have told the teacher."

Gramps then told me, "There is a practical solution and an emotional solution. If you tell the teacher and she moves your seat, you have solved the practical problem of avoiding the situation. Sometimes the practical solution is the best and it might have been in this situation. What would the emotional solution be?"

"I'm not sure," I responded.

"Ah, the emotional solution is thinking differently about the situation. You told me you have been able to do this. How could you apply it here?"

"Alright, I should have kept in mind on my goals to have friends and not getting angry. I should have told myself that I don't like Don kicking my seat, but I can stand it since I stood it the previous two days. I should have told myself that it wasn't awful because awful would be getting hit over the head with a baseball bat."

"What should Don have done?" Gramps asked.

"I should have expected him to act like himself and that was to squirm around and kick chairs."

"Yes," Gramps replied, "if you would have done all of that logical thinking, you probably would not have gotten angry and been able to think better about how to solve the problem. Now, given that Don is a hyperactive boy, you probably couldn't have reasoned with him or stopped his behavior. Even after putting him on the floor, you didn't teach him anything, except that he probably thinks that you are a mean kid now. So, the only appropriate solution is to calmly tell the teacher that you are having a hard time concentrating in class with Don kicking your seat and ask her if there is any way that you or maybe Don could sit somewhere else. Since the teacher wants you to concentrate in class, I'm thinking she would have gladly accommodated you if you asked nicely."

"Makes sense, Gramps. I'll continue to work on this. I really want to act in ways that support my goals."

"Now, what has four wheels and flies?" Gramps asked.

"Hey. I've heard that one before, and I know the answer is a garbage truck, but I don't get it because garbage trucks don't fly," I responded.

Gramps laughed and said, "No, but those little flying insects like to hang around garage trucks, so it has four and wheels and also has flies."

I laughed. "Now it makes sense. Let me ask you about another joke. I thought the joke about the newspaper was strange. I know the Spinal Column has a pink cover, but why is a newspaper black and white and red all over?"

Gramps laughed when I asked about this joke. "I doubt the joke is about the Spinal Column. What do you do with a newspaper?"

"Well, I read the sports section and throw the rest out."

"You *read* the paper? What did you do to Sunday's newspaper?"

"I read it, well, at least the sports page."

"So, if a lot of people *read* the newspaper on Sunday, you could say...?"

"Ah, it was read all over." I laughed out loud. I finally understood a couple classic jokes.

The Baseball Bat

"Hello, I love you.
Won't you tell me your name?
Hello, I love you.
Let me jump in your game."
— The Doors (1968)

A Glance

On Saturday, we beat the Indians. I got a solid hit, but also struck out for the first time that season. I wondered how I would react when I struck out. Some players slam the baseball bat down, some say something under their breath and others just walk back to the bench. I don't strike out much. I like to hit the first good pitch because I want to have as few pitches as possible to lower my chance of getting hit by the pitch. After fouling off two pitches, I swung and missed at a pitch that might have been too high. You might think with my history that I would have chosen a more violent reaction, but I just walked back to the bench similarly to how I had walked up to bat.

I heard Coach say, "Tom, you took some good cuts at the ball."

My thoughts were that there was no one to blame, so why be mad? I had done a good job putting the ball in play all year. Maybe I surprised some people with my calm reaction. I know my mother was probably holding her breath. Maybe some players need to do crazy things and yell to let everyone know they can do better. I prefer drawing little attention to myself with something embarrassing.

In my last at bat of the game, I had thought about bunting after the strike out, but I hadn't practiced bunting very much. It is difficult to practice bunting when my main source of batting practice had been hitting rocks I had tossed up in the air. The first pitch came right toward me. I turned, and the ball hit me in the back. I had seen other boys hit the ground crying when this happened, but I was not going to do that. I just stood there for a minute, assessing whether I was still alive and could still breathe.

I heard the umpire yell, "Take your base."

I took off running to first because I saw Coach coming out to check on me. I wanted to avoid Coach treating me like a child. I wanted to be a man about this situation. When I got to first, the first base coach looked at me and asked if I was okay.

I looked at him and said, "I'm fine," even though I could feel my back hurting.

I wasn't planning on stealing, but the next pitch got by the catcher, so I took off for second. In my Mustang League method of official scoring, that was a stolen base. As it turns out, there were two more balls that got by the catcher, that got me to third and home, all stolen bases in my scoring system. We won the game 7-6, with my run being the seventh and winning run.

After the game, I was congratulated more for "taking one for the team," meaning getting hit, and possibly hurt on purpose, and eventually scoring than I did for my solid hit earlier and my good play at first base. I was even asked if I got hit deliberately to get the winning run on base. I decided to just go with it and say yes, we needed the runner, so I took the pitch. The truth was I certainly didn't get hit on purpose this time or at any time throughout my baseball career, but if this is what makes me the hero, going along with it was my best choice. As it turns out, it was the only time I got hit by the pitch all year. I did have a ball mark on my back for several days, but it went away.

I talked to Stan a little after the game and we congratulated each other. He told me that there wasn't going to be the neighborhood game on Sunday. He said he would let me know about the date of the next one. I really wanted Stan to be my friend, so I tended to be overly friendly towards him. I decided to try a joke with him and asked, "How do you catch a bear?"

I paused, and then said, "Cut a hole in the ice and put a bunch of peas around it and when the bear comes to take a pea, kick him in the hole." I had forgotten about the "ice hole."

He laughed and then had one for me. "Okay, why is nine afraid of seven? Because seven, eight, nine."

We both laughed.

After getting back from the grocery store where I begged my mother for Ding Dongs, I asked to go down to the lake. Gramps was out washing his truck, so I asked him if I could take a boat out. Gramps agreed, but first asked how the game went. I told him how I had scored the winning run. I rowed around the lake close to shore when I spotted this girl who I thought was very beautiful. She looked about my age; I had never seen her before. She was sitting out in a lounge chair in a blue, flowered bikini with her hair parted down the middle, which flowed almost to her waist. She looked at me. I quickly looked away and just kept rowing. I couldn't stop thinking about her. Who was she? Why hadn't I seen her before? What school did she attend?

I got back and pulled the boat up on shore. I went over and asked Gramps who lived in the big house with the white brick and the dock.

Gramps said, "Oh that is where Doris and Hank live. Hank likes to have his children and grandchildren out on weekends."

"Gramps, I just saw the girl of my dreams there."

"She must be one of Hank's grandchildren who live out in Livonia. Maybe she is visiting this weekend. Did you talk to her? Did you offer her a ride?"

"No, she is beautiful. How could I talk to a girl that beautiful?"

"How do you talk to ordinary girls?"

"Hmmm," I thought about this and said, "I guess it is easier because I don't have to worry about blowing it with a possible girlfriend."

Gramps said, "Hmmm, so by not talking to her, you have a better chance of having her as your girlfriend?"

As usual, Gramps provided solid logic. I headed home, thinking about what he had said.

On Saturday night, my mother wanted me to spend some time with Grandma and Grandpa Mochina. I asked her, "So, are you going out with

Mr. Pete? By the way, is that his last name or his first name?"

My mother replied, "Hmmm, I assumed it was his first name, but I'm not sure. His truck has a sign, Pete's Electrical. Maybe it's his last name. Yes, he asked me out again."

I wanted to say a few more derogatory things, but I decided to only say, "Maybe his name is Peter Pete."

It was good catching up with my grandparents and hearing about how the Detroit Tigers were in first place. Grandpa Mochina told me the Tigers had won big again, 12-2, but he talked more about the weird tie game the night before, when the umpires had to call the game after 7 innings with the score tied 2-2. He told me that they didn't finish the game, but the game counted as a tie, each player's statistics counted toward their season totals and still played a make-up game. This rule of having tie games is not in existence today.

On Sunday, I thought another rowboat ride was in order, and Gramps kindly obliged me. I rowed over to the same house but this time, no one was outside. I still didn't have a plan of what I was going to say. Maybe if she saw me, she would want to start a conversation with me. I rowed back and spent the rest of the day listening to music. I somehow found this dream girl in the lyrics of almost every song.

The Baseball Bat

"Come along if you care.
Come along if you dare.
Take a ride to the land inside of your mind."
— The Amboy Dukes (1968)

Focus on Grades

On Monday, I decided I needed practice talking to girls. I decided to start with some girls that were average-looking. I noticed that Karen was now sitting in front of Don, and he was kicking her seat. She looked annoyed. At lunch, I approached her and asked how she liked the new seating arrangement.

Karen responded, "Would you please dump that moron, Don, on his head again?"

I guess I set myself up for her question. I told her, "No, if I do that again, I'll be in big trouble. I bet if you said something to the teacher, she would finally understand and move him to the first row."

Wow, I was now giving advice that didn't include taking some kind of action into my own hands. I knew I was lucky by only getting a warning when I had flipped Don's desk. Karen did talk to the teacher and got Don moved to the front row. I wish I had handled it that way when I had the chance.

Later that day, I saw Lori studying, so I approached her. Lori got all A's and was pretty much thought of as the smartest student in the class.

"Hi, Lori," I said, "Are you all set for the math and spelling tests tomorrow?"

"Hi, Tom," she said, "I am all set for math, but have a little more studying to do on spelling. There are some tricky words like theory, friend and literature, but I'll have them by tomorrow.

In my mind, the competition was on. The goal of talking to girls became secondary to the goal of who could get the best grades. I didn't like that anyone could be considered smarter than me. I got off the bus that day and checked in with Carol, and told her I had some homework to do. Ordinarily, the only time that I stayed in her house was a bad weather day, and today the sun was shining brightly. I first tackled the spelling words. I spoke theory as three syllables: thee-or-ee, and said it several times. I spoke friend in two syllables: fry-end. With literature, I spoke this slowly saying four syllables: lit-er-a-ture. I asked Carol to read me the words from the list as I wrote them. I then checked my work and I had gotten them all correct.

Next, I went over the math problems. I had to add and subtract fractions together with different denominators. I knew the concept of finding the common denominator, but if I rushed, I might write down the incorrect numerator when changing the denominator. I spent a little extra time and checked my work. I think I had the process of checking my work down, so I had to remember the goal was getting a 100 and not necessarily handing my test in first.

The next day, we took the tests in the morning. I took my time and checked my work. I felt pretty good about them. After lunch, the teacher put the grades indicated by percentages on the board. The percent sign was not used. For spelling, there were three 100s, three 90s, one 80, five 70s, six 60s and two 50 or below. For math, there was one 100, one 95, three 90s and the rest below 90. I felt pretty good that I had the 100 in spelling. How could I have made a mistake in math? I'm assuming Lori got the 100. The teacher handed back the spelling tests. Yes, I got a 100! I decided I should forever call my friends, fry-ends and say literature as four syllables. I was excited.

The teacher then handed back the math tests face down. Before turning my paper over, I breathed a few times and shut my eyes. I said to myself that I would be okay with whatever grade I got. I slowly turned the paper a little and saw the 100 and a smiley face. I kept it face down and just breathed. Then I glanced over at Lori. She didn't look very happy. Then, she started looking around the room to see who was celebrating the 100, but I didn't smile and tried not to look at her.

After class, she started asking the better students how they had done. I was the third person she asked. "Tom, how did you do on the math test?"

"Oh, I'm pretty good at fractions," I said softly and confidently, "I got a 100. How did you do?"

"I thought I knew fractions well too, but I made a stupid mistake on one problem."

Although I was celebrating the victory over Lori inside, I did not let it show on the outside. I had created a game between us, and she didn't even know I was determined to beat her. There were only four weeks left in the fourth grade, but I had committed myself to turning every test into a competition and trying to finish the last grading period strongly.

That evening, we had our game against the Braves and were now 5 wins with only 2 losses after beating them soundly. I played a good first base and the parents still shouted, "The Machine." I had two more hits. Stan and Joe each had homeruns in the game. Stan now had two homeruns, Joe had one and Will had hit one in an earlier game. No wonder they are batting 2-3-4. I really wanted to hit a homerun, but the Coach had asked me to try to swing even and hit line drives. I just couldn't help but think that the Detroit Tigers were famous for hitting homeruns. I walked away from that win unsatisfied, even though I had had a good game.

On Thursday evening, we got beat by the Yankees. It was my first at bat against their pitcher, who had a very herky-jerky motion. I tried to swing a lot harder with a little upper cut. It didn't work; I struck out. I ended up going 0 for 3 that day. I probably shouldn't have tried to change my swing because I was having success. I also probably picked the wrong pitcher with whom to change my batting approach.

On Friday, we had our Social Studies test. I again studied really hard and got a 100. There were four 100s in the class and Lori again checked with me to see how I had done. I shared my grade with her, and she wanted me to know that she had gotten a 100 as well. The competition was on. I wish I had started this back in September.

— ✦ —

On Friday after school, I took a trip down the hill and Gramps was out working near the lake. I walked toward him and heard the familiar, "Tommy Boy," he said, "I haven't seen you much this week."

"Gramps, how are you doing?"

"Life can't get any better for me. I live by this beautiful lake, have a great wife, get to work at the greatest university, get to look out on the lake and see girls in bikinis and get to talk to you," Gramps said, as he smiled.

I had come down to talk to him about some things, but got sidetracked when he said bikini. "Where are the bikini girls?" I asked.

"Oh, they will be out over the weekend and just wait until school lets out. They will be out every day."

On Saturday, we played against the Tigers, which I found really odd. How did this team get to be the called the Tigers? Stan knew a few guys on the Tigers, and they told him that they were 8-0. We were supposed to play them earlier in the season, but the game had gotten rained out. The Tigers had twin pitchers. Both were short with almost white hair and both threw hard. We had to face both in this game. They beat us 7-2. I played a good first base. I tried to get back to my swing that had been successful, but I didn't get a hit. I did walk once and stole a base. We were now five wins and four losses on the year. Stan asked me to come over and go to the neighborhood game on Sunday, so I agreed. Even though I didn't do well in the last neighborhood game, I had a chance to hang with

Stan, so I accepted the invitation. As it turned out, I didn't do a whole lot better, but I had fun.

After going with my mother to the grocery store and laundromat, I headed down the hill, but not to look for Gramps this time. I was looking for bikinis and possibly the dream girl that I had seen down the lake. I saw Gramps and asked if I could row a boat, and he happily agreed. I grabbed some cushions from the boathouse and rowed down the lake, but no one was out at Hank's house. I kept rowing and saw girls in bikinis in motorboats on the lake. One girl in her late teens waved when she saw me, and I returned the wave. I thought about what Gramps said about life. Life was pretty good for me too. I was out on the lake on a bright, sunshiny day, getting exercise and looking at pretty girls.

The next week at school, I continued to work really hard at getting good grades and to try to let the little things not bother me using the thinking strategies that Gramps had taught me. We played two games that week instead of three because of one rainout. I had a great week at the plate going 5 for 6 with one double, 6 RBIs and 4 stolen bases. I played a solid first base and made a scoop putout at first in each game. We were happy about getting the wins. I had played every inning of every game at first base. No one else had played my position. We won both games and our record was now 7-4. With only three games left, this guaranteed us at least a .500 season. There was one of the rainout games that we were not able to make up, so we played 14 games instead of 15 that season. It was going to be tough during the last week of the season having to play the undefeated Tigers twice and the Yankees once.

On Saturday night, we went to my grandparents' house. As usual, I got the update on the Detroit Tigers. They had won again with Denny McLain pitching. Denny was now 7-1 on the season. My mother did not go out and just stayed and visited with her parents. Maybe it was over with Mr. Pete—at least I hoped.

The Baseball Bat

"Sloopy lives in very bad part of town.
And everybody, yeah,
tries to put my Sloopy down."
— The McCoys (1965)

Low Times

O n Tuesday, we played the makeup game with the Tigers. We were trailing 8-1 in the top of the fifth inning. We only played six innings in the Mustang League. I led off the inning. I hadn't had much luck against the twin pitchers, so I decided to take a couple pitches and they were both called balls. I took the next three pitches and drew a walk. This was probably the first time all season that I had come up to the plate and not swung the baseball bat, except for the time I got hit by the pitch.

Coach told us that because we were so far behind, and the Tigers had a strong throwing catcher, to not try to steal unless we knew we could make it. I didn't run on the first pitch, but just observed to see if I could make it on the second pitch. I was sure I could steal second pitch. On the next pitch as soon as the ball crossed the plate, I took off running as fast as I could and slid into second base.

After I had touched the base, the second baseman tagged me and I heard the umpire yell, "You're OUT."

What? I thought. I was clearly safe. What was wrong with this umpire? I stood up on the base and yelled, "You're crazy!" and stayed on the base.

Then the umpire yelled, "You're out of the game!"

My heart sunk. I put my head down, fighting back the tears, as I walked back to the bench. Everyone could tell how upset I was, and no one said a word to me. I just sat there with my head down.

After that inning, Coach asked Stan to take first and Mark to play shortstop. If I had to give up one inning at first base, I was glad it was to Stan. We lost 10-1. I guess Coach made the decision not to pitch Stan because we were behind, and he wanted to save him for the last two games. After the game, I didn't talk to anyone and just walked to the car. I heard someone try to tell the story, and they reported that I had told the umpire that he was full of crap. I didn't correct him and got in the car and left.

Getting thrown out of the game really bothered me. I wish I had reacted in a different way. On Wednesday, I went down the hill to see if I could find Gramps, and lucky for me, he was out. I told Gramps what had happened.

"Tom, you are doing so much better. You are only getting angry a fraction of the times you were. However, every once in awhile, things get to us, and you can't beat yourself up for it. No, it was not good to yell at the umpire, but it happened."

"Gramps, how can I ever recover from this? I had tried to have such a good season, and now everyone saw me get angry."

"So, Tom, this is the end of the world? This is worse than getting hit over the head with a baseball bat?"

"This time, I did something I can't recover from. I'm marked for life."

"Oh, no! I wish I had known this! When I was young, I got kicked out of three baseball games and a basketball game. I'm glad I didn't know that life was over when those events happened because I would have never been able to buy this lake house."

I was surprised to hear that Gramps had been kicked out of games. I have never seen him even close to getting angry.

"Tom, I was an angry kid growing up, and I didn't have anyone to help me learn to control my anger. I had to learn it on my own. I wish I had known half of what you know now when I was 10-years-old."

I thought for minute about this and asked, "How do I recover from this?"

"Tom, you have three options. First, you can feel bad about it for the rest of your life and sulk and not talk to anyone. Second, you can admit you made a mistake to yourself and just try to do the best you can tomorrow. Third, you can take a bad event and try to make it a positive."

I listened to the options and replied, "Option 2 certainly sounds better than option 1 when you put it that way. How could I accomplish Option 3?"

"You can call your Coach, and admit to him that you did something you regret and let your team down in the process. You can then tell him that the team means a lot to you, and you are going to do everything you can to help your team in the future. If you really wanted to make it a positive, you could ask the coach if you could take a moment before the next game to apologize to your teammates."

"How would that be a positive?"

"Because you would show your maturity. You would show that you are human and you make mistakes, but you don't think you are better than all others. You would show that you are not going to hide behind defensiveness. Defensiveness attempts to show that the umpire was wrong and you were right. You will find in life that it's not a good thing to try to show people they are wrong because all that does is damage relationships. Tom, you will find that relationships are the most valuable asset you will ever have. Most importantly, you would show you are willing to accept responsibility for your actions."

"Wouldn't this make me weak?"

"Tom, being an honest, genuine person who can admit mistakes makes you a very strong person."

I thanked Gramps for his help and felt somewhat better as I headed home.

That night, I called Coach and told him that the team meant a lot to me, and I was genuinely sorry for my actions. I also asked if I could address the team before the game on Thursday.

Coach said, "Tom, I have enjoyed having you on the team all year. I would be happy to let you address the team."

The next day was Memorial Day, Thursday, May 30th. Back in 1968, Memorial Day was still celebrated on May 30th. The Uniform Monday Holiday Act of 1968 would change this to Memorial Day always be celebrated on a Monday, starting in 1971. My teacher had talked to us about Memorial Day, and said that we should remember those who had given their lives for country. I wanted to live a long life and wondered if some day I would have to serve in the military. It frightened me to think about it. My mother didn't have to work on Memorial Day, and I didn't have to go to school, so my mother took me to a Memorial Day parade in Walled Lake. It was fun; I got some free candy.

—◆—

Thursday night came. As usual, I was one of the first to arrive along with Stan and Coach. Stan and I started to loosen up a little by playing catch. About five minutes before the start of the game, Coach called the players in and told them to play their best today, and then he turned to me and said, "Tom."

I looked at the players very sadly and said, "I have really enjoyed being part of this team. I have worked hard and tried to help us win games. On Tuesday, I not only contributed to the loss, but

I embarrassed myself and the team. I'm sorry. I will try my best not to embarrass the team again. Thank you."

I waited a second, and then one person started clapping, and then everyone on the team started clapping. Then Coach told us to go to our positions, and I started throwing ground balls to the infield as Joe was warming up pitching. I did not know what to expect, but the clapping far exceeded my expectations.

We played a tough game against the second place team, the Yankees. We were trailing 6-4 in the bottom of the sixth inning. Joe had gotten on first via a walk and had stolen second, but both Will and Paul had struck out. It was all up to me with two outs in the bottom of the sixth inning. As I approached the plate knowing that I could be the last out, I kept telling myself to be calm and do my best. I had the thought that making an out would not compare to being hit over the head with a baseball bat. I just tried to focus and do my best to hit the ball.

On the first pitch, I hit the ball hard on the ground and it traveled out to center field, and Joe came in to score. We were trailing only by one run now and I was at first base. Do I try to steal second to try to get the tying run to second and risk being the last out of the game? I looked over to Coach for guidance. All he said was, "Okay, Tom, be smart."

What did that mean? The next batter, Jeff, who had come on to play left field in the fourth inning, took the first pitch for a called strike, and I stayed at first. The next pitch was also a called strike, and I again stayed at first. I decided I was only going to go if the next pitch was in the dirt. The next pitch was in the dirt, but Jeff had swung at it and missed for the final out. The Mustang League does not allow players to run to first on a strike out when the catcher doesn't catch the ball so the game was over.

I wish I could have done more. It was disappointing to lose by one run. What else could I have done? I could have been the last out, and that would have been worse. I finally decided I had kept the team in the game by getting a base hit and felt good about that.

The Baseball Bat

> *"It's a beautiful morning. Ahhh.*
> *I think I'll go outside for awhile,*
> *And just smile*
> *Just take in some clean fresh air, boy."*
> — *The Rascals (1968)*

Better Times

I t was June 1, 1968, the last game of season.
We played the Tigers, who had gone through
the season undefeated by the strength of their
twin pitchers. One twin would pitch the first three
innings, and the other one would pitch the last
three innings. Both threw the ball very hard. We
never faced their other pitchers in the three games
that we played against the Tigers.

The Tigers were up 5-3 in the bottom of the
sixth inning. We had the top of the order up. Our
leadoff hitter, Art, got hit by the pitch, and he said
something that we all assumed was in Korean as
he trotted down to first base. Art stole second on
the first pitch. Stan then hit a ground ball to the
third baseman. The third baseman looked Art back
to second and then tried to throw to first base, but
the throw pulled the first baseman off the bag. Art
hustled to third on the throw to first.

Stan stole second on the first pitch, and we
had the tying runs at second and third with
nobody out. We were in a good position to at least
tie the game.

We had two strong hitters coming up. Our
third hitter, Joe, had hit pretty well all year. He
went up to the plate and swung at the first three
pitches, but never connected and struck out. It was
disappointing, but there was only one out. Will

was up next and he was a strong hitter too. I wished it were me up there in the fourth spot in the order. Will had seen Joe strike out and took a more conservative approach by taking the first pitch; it was called a ball. He ended up walking on four pitches to load the bases.

So, it was up to Paul, with one out and the bases loaded. Paul took the first pitch, but it was called a strike. He then took three more pitches to get the count was 2 balls and 2 strikes. On the next pitch he swung, but never came close to hitting the twin's fastball and struck out.

Now, it was up to me, with two outs and the bases loaded. This was my opportunity to realize a dream of getting a hit to tie, or even win, the game. I also thought about how bad it would be if I made the last out to lose the game. As I took the donut off my bat, I remembered Gramps telling me that "if you get a chance to be a star, make sure you give it your best effort, but stay relaxed and focused, and if you don't come through, it's not the end of the world." I felt confident because I was able to get a hit in a similar situation on Thursday.

I stepped up to the batter's box, and in my usual fashion, was ready to hit the first pitch. I was not going to try to wait for a walk like some of the other players might have done. I'm sure many parents were hoping for a walk. I even heard my coach yell, "make it be in there," so I guess he would be happy for a walk too.

I heard the Tiger's coach say, "Get the batter. All we need is one more out."

I dug in, ready to hit, but the first pitch was inside, and I moved out of the way.

"Ball one," roared the umpire.

92

Luckily for me, this was a different umpire then I had on Tuesday.

I could hear my coach say, "Good eye now." Probably most of our parents were hoping I would just walk, or that there would be a couple wild pitches to help get the tying runs across.

I dug in again, and was ready to swing hard if it was a pitch near the plate. The next pitch was low and away, but not far off the plate. I swung and connected solidly, driving a line drive over the second baseman's head. I took off running as fast I could. The first base coach told me to keep running, and I did, as fast as I could. As I rounded first, I saw the outfielders still chasing the ball into the higher grass. I rounded second base and could see a couple runs had already scored, so I just kept going. I never even looked at the third base coach as I approached third base. I never slowed down and just kept running to home. As the ball was coming into the infield, the Tiger players knew they had already lost, but the pitcher fired the ball home anyway. The throw was too late for the catcher to try to tag me. I didn't slide. I just kept running full speed across home plate.

As I crossed the plate, the players and coaches were jumping up and down. Here was my chance. I could jump around like the rest of them if I wanted, but I didn't. It had already been an emotional week for me. I had just hit my first homerun, but I took the attitude that this is how I should hit and can do even better. I celebrated in my mind, but was calm on the outside. I never saw Norm Cash or Bill Freehan jumping around because for them it was just another homerun of many. I wanted to show everyone that this should just be the normal for me as well.

It felt like we had just won the World Series because we beat the undefeated team. I graciously accepted all the "great hit" comments from both teams, and many of the parents, as my teammates kept jumping around and yelling.

One parent even said to me, "Aren't you excited?"

"I'm excited," I said, "I did my job." I guess the parents were expecting more from the emotional kid who called the umpire crazy.

For those who know baseball, understand that officially it was not a homerun. Officially, the game was over when the winning run crossed the plate. The winning run was Will and as soon as he scored, the game was over. If I hadn't touched third base when he touched home, an official scorer would have awarded me a double. However, most people in attendance didn't know the official scoring rules, so most thought it was a homerun. When I got home, I entered my stats, and I certainly recorded the hit as a homerun with four RBIs. I controlled my stats, and I decided I wanted to see a homerun as part of my permanent statistics instead of double.

After the game, the coach treated us all to ice cream at the local Dairy Queen. There was only vanilla back then, but he did allow us to get our vanilla cones dipped in chocolate. My plate appearance was the last at bat of the season for this team. I made a lasting impression on everyone. No matter what happened throughout the season, I was remembered for the "grand slam homerun" to beat the undefeated Tigers. I had made a recovery from the Tuesday night incident just like Gramps had told me. I just couldn't help but think this was going to be the first homerun of many to come, and I dreamed about the future. Yes, my life wasn't over after my outburst. I made a mistake, but life went on.

My mother decided to let Saturday be my day, and she did the grocery shopping and laundry on Sunday. She told me that we would be going to the Big Boy in Walled Lake for dinner that evening and asked if I would like to take a friend. Wow, I had never been to a dine-in restaurant with waitresses. This was really special to me. I had only previously been to Arby's and McDonald's, neither of which had waitresses. I called Stan and worked out a time to pick him up to go to Big Boy. I'm sure Stan had dined at many restaurants in his life, but we were going to celebrate tonight.

Not having to go on the weekly trips, I headed down to the lake. Gramps was down there trimming some trees. I approached him, and the first thing I said was, "Gramps, I think I recovered."

Gramps smiled.

"On Wednesday, I called the coach and then addressed the team on Thursday. We ended up losing Thursday by one run. I was on base and I could have been the tying run, but the next guy up struck out. Then we had to play the undefeated team again today. It was really tough. We trailed 5-3 with two outs and the bases loaded in the bottom of the sixth inning, and I was up." I said with a frown. Then I smiled and my voice got louder. "I hit a grand slam homerun to win the game."

Gramps said, "Oh, I am so proud of you. That is great."

"Thanks Gramps," I said, as I got more quiet and serious, "You helped me. It's baseball, so there was a chance that I would have made the last out. I knew this as I walked up to the plate, so I just tried to stay relaxed, do my best and not get down if I wasn't successful. I think staying calm and not worrying really helped me to concentrate on the ball." I got a little louder and more excited. "It feels really great. It was an up and down season, but it ended on a high note. We finished 8-6, which seems a whole lot better than the 7-7 record we would have had if I had made the last out."

Gramps replied, "It's good to celebrate wins and grieve losses. Today, we celebrate." Gramps had put an old steel outdoor chair, one you might see at an old gas station, out at the end of the dock. "Hey Tom, I put the chair at the end of the dock, so we could get a closer look when the girls in the bikinis boat by," said Gramps with a smile.

That night, my mother and I went to pick up Stan, and we went to Big Boy. I didn't really want to tell Stan that it was my first time at a dine-in restaurant. I asked my mother not to tell him. We had fun and talked a lot about the game.

Stan was excited about the game. "We beat the Tigers. They were all set to celebrate their undefeated season, and we took it away from them. It was a game I will never forget. Since I had only pitched 3 innings this week, and Joe and Will had already pitched their 6 innings, I knew I had to pitch against the best team, and we were already down, 5-1. I was so happy to pitch so well today and keep us in the game."

"Stan, you pitched so well all year, but you pitched great today. You have hit so well all year too," I said, and for the first time I realized that the game today wasn't all about me. Stan was just as important as me, if not much more.

Stan went on, "I wasn't happy about the way I hit the ball in the sixth inning, but I was happy to get on base, so we still had a chance. I really felt Joe would drive home Art and me to tie the game, but then he struck out and Will walked. When Paul struck out, I looked and saw you coming up. You really looked confident. Weren't you nervous at all?"

"I sure was nervous, but I tried to stay relaxed and focused on hitting the ball."

"You really smacked it! As soon as I saw the ball hit the ground in the outfield, I raced for home and then turned and cheered for Will to score. It was really exciting!"

Stan and I kept talking about the game throughout dinner. We had a lot of fun and laughed a lot while we were together. I think Stan thought that I had finally emerged as a baseball player and was someone who could be a solid teammate of his in any sport. I also think that Stan appreciated that I was academically smart unlike most of his neighborhood friends. However, there was one secret that I kept from Stan. I hadn't had him over to my house because then he would know that I lived in one of the smallest houses in the area.

When I got home, I entered my statistics for the final game. For my season, I hit .425 with one homerun, 18 RBIs, two doubles, 7 runs scored and

14 stolen bases. It was fun for me to keep these stats because probably everyone else in the league just kept some stats in their head. Any major leaguer who had these statistics in only 14 games would be elated.

Sometimes, I reflected on how I had all zeros the previous season. I did absolutely nothing. How did I have the 180 degrees turnaround? I think it was just mainly through my determination to do well and all of the time I spent with the pitch back net and hitting rocks. Maybe my overconfidence helped me in some way to play better than I actually was. Stan had close to double the numbers that I did this year, but he had played much longer than I had. Could I be as good as Stan some day? My goal was to be the best, and so someday I would like to match his numbers. I hoped to play a lot more seasons with my new friend. Could I now do anything I set my mind to accomplish? This season had given me a lot of confidence. This day will always be special, but I hoped there would be a lot more special days to come.

"I'm sittin' on the dock of the bay
watching the tide roll away.
Oooo, I'm sittin' on the dock of the bay
wastin' time."
— Otis Redding (1968)

Creating Calm

O n Monday, we started our last week of
school. I was still focused hard on getting
good grades, and I wanted to finish the
year strong. As I sat in class, I heard the loud,
intermittent, annoying sound of the alert siren.
The teacher instructed us to quickly line up, and
she guided us to the hallway. She had us sit cross-
legged against the wall, with our hands folded
behind our backs of heads and our heads down in
our lap. This was an uncomfortable position for
me. I wasn't designed to bend this way. Why did
we have to do this drill on the last week of school?
Maybe it was real. Maybe we were being bombed
by the Soviet Union. I couldn't wait until Bobby
Kennedy got to be president, so he could end the
Cold War. Maybe this was an earthquake or a
tornado. A lot of thoughts ran through my head;
then the bell rang. It was over. It was just a drill.

We had tests in all of our subjects because it
was the last week of school. The teacher had
spread them out to have tests in English and social
studies on Tuesday with science and spelling and
math on Wednesday. Thursday would just be a
party. Of course, much of the conversation that
day was about the game. Yes, *the* game, the 13-0
Tigers against the 7-6 Cardinals. Later in the fall,

the Detroit Tigers ended up playing the St. Louis Cardinals in the World Series, but the game of the day was the Mustang League game that I played in and got the winning hit.

Everyone had their own version of the game. Will had a version in which he scored the winning run. Everyone on the team was able to celebrate the victory in his own way. We each put our own slant on the game. It was just a Mustang League game, but for those of us on the Cardinals, it was a huge part of our lives.

I saw Lori, who was talking to Karen, and she looked up at me and said, "Tom, are you ready for the tests?"

"I don't think I am quite ready. It was such a wild weekend with the game. How are you going to study for the final tests?"

"For English, you have to be able to determine all of the parts of the sentence. If I were you, I would go over the practice sheets and try some sentences from the book. For Social Studies, just practice the state facts," she said.

"I'll do my best."

When I got home from school each day, I went to Carol's house and studied for the tests until my mother got home. In class, I took my time and checked my work. The big game was over, but there was a new game this week called academics, and I wanted to win this game too.

On Wednesday, we first got our English test back. There were only two 100s and when I turned my paper over, I got one of them. Then the teacher handed back the social studies test and again there were two 100s. I turned mine over and I had gotten a 90. I got confused on the state motto of Texas. I put "With God all things are possible," but that was the state motto of Ohio. The Texas motto is "Friendship." I got confused again by putting Indiana as the Christmas Tree Capitol of the World, but it was Indiana County, Pennsylvania. How confusing! I didn't get too upset with my 90, but I wanted to do better in the future, so I decided that I needed more time to study for social studies. I did wonder who got the 100s, but I never found out.

I studied for the final three tests and tried to ace them. I ended up getting a 100 on the last spelling test, a 95 on the science test and a 100 on the math test. I will never forget that it is the praying mantis that flies like a humming bird and not the moth because that was the question I missed on the science test. The final grades would be mailed to us. I knew I would get an S (Satisfactory) in art, music and gym, because I gave a lot of effort in all three. Did I do well enough to get all A's this grading period?

After we took our tests on Wednesday, June 5th, our teacher reported to us that presidential candidate, Bobby Kennedy, had been shot and was in critical condition. I was sure that Bobby Kennedy was going to win the presidency. I probably didn't have any sound political reason for this statement. I guess I was thinking more about the presidency running in families. I remember seeing that he had just won the California primary. I remember watching some of his speeches, especially the one when he announced the assassination of Martin Luther King, Jr. I decided that day that it was unsafe to ever be president, so I would no longer have that dream. We got the word the next day that he had died.

On Thursday, it was the end of the year party. This was more special to me than anyone else because I missed this party in the third grade. We played games all day and ate cookies. It was a fun day. I loved playing all sorts of games, and I had that competitiveness about me. I watched as people said goodbye to each other for the summer and saw the sadness they felt. It was hard for me to understand. I felt happy that I wouldn't have to see many of them for a while, especially those who had crossed me. I took the bus home for the last time as a fourth grader. I was not going to miss riding the bus all summer, either. I did think that for fifth grade, I would try harder to tolerate the bus, because I had no other way of getting to school.

I got home and checked in with Carol and asked if I could go to the lake. I went down the hill and didn't see Gramps, so I went on the dock and sat in the chair that he had put on the end of the dock. I sat there and it felt so peaceful. There weren't a lot of boats going by, but I just sat there and watched the water and birds.

After a little while, Gramps came out and walked out on the dock.

"Tommy Boy, the wife had some things for me to do in the house, and I like to keep her happy."

"Hi, Gramps."

"Do you feel peaceful sitting in the chair looking out at the water?"

"Gramps, this is about as peaceful as I can imagine it."

"For me, this is true peace, and you know something, Tom? I can take this with me wherever I go."

"Take it with you?"

"Yes, I can recreate this scene in my mind whenever I need to do it. For instance, just now, my wife had me scrubbing the toilet, but in my mind, I was picturing looking out at the lake and time went by faster."

Instead of understanding the point, I couldn't help but laugh at the word toilet.

Gramps continued, "In April, I started to get stressed out when trying to figure out my taxes, so I decided to recreate this scene, and I was at peace. When I gave the grades out to my medical students, some of them got upset because they were expecting higher grades. Instead of letting this get to me, I recreated this scene of looking out at the calm lake, and I felt calmness. Try it when you get home."

"I will," I said with a smile, "but for now, I better take more of it in."

— ✦ —

I went back home and sat on the porch until my mother got home. When she came in the house, she asked me about my last day of school, we had dinner and then we discussed the plans for the summer. She told me that I would have to stay with my grandparents again for the summer. What a disappointment! I started to whine.

"But Mom, I don't want to go to the city. There is nothing to do there. I want to be by the lake. I want to be home with my toys and my music."

"Tom, you are only 10-years-old. I cannot leave you alone"

"I'm not going," I replied harshly.

"Tom, your grandparents are expecting you tomorrow."

I just sat and pouted. Finally I decided to turn the television on to watch the Thursday ABC line up of *The Flying Nun*, *Bewitched* and *That Girl*. All of these actresses were attractive, but there was something special about Sally Fields, the star of *The Flying Nun*. I remember when the show first came out, I thought it was the flying nut because I was Protestant, and I had never heard the word nun before.

It was Friday morning, and I wasn't happy with the arrangement about having to go to the city, so I went, but I hardly said a word to my mother. I didn't speak much to my grandparents either. Finally, my grandfather asked me about my last baseball game. I told him about hitting the game winning grand slam homerun, and it made me smile a little.

My grandfather said, "So, it seems that you really didn't want to come here today?"

"I appreciate you having me, but I really enjoy being at the lake."

Then I remembered what Gramps had told me. I could be on the end of the dock any time in my mind, so I decided to try it. After about five minutes, I felt much better.

I smiled and asked my grandfather how the Detroit Tigers were doing.

"We just beat Boston 3 out 5. On Wednesday, Denny McLain got his ninth win of the year. They brought in veteran Eddie Matthews to bat for him, and Eddie got a base hit. Since

Eddie is getting old, the coach decided to use a pinch runner and he decided on Micky Lolich. I never thought I would see the day that Lolich was used as a pinch run. He is so fat. Tom, you could run faster than Lolich."

The rest of the day went better, but I was happy when I finally got to be home.

The Baseball Bat

*"Sometimes I wonder
what I'm going to do.
Lord, there ain't no cure
for the summertime blues."
— Blue Cheer (1967)*

Start of Summer

O n Saturday, I asked my mother if we could go early to the laundromat and the grocery store, so I could enjoy the warm weather down by the lake, and she was more than happy to get going early. When we got back, I headed down to the lake. I saw Gramps out and told him about me having to go into the city during the week to stay with my grandparents and my poor attitude toward it, but that I tried the imaging technique he taught me.

"Good, I'm glad you remembered to try it."

"Tom, I have another technique if you are interested."

"Of course, you have taught me so much. I want to learn more."

"How much did it help to sulk?" he asked.

"Hmmm, well, I guess I showed my mother I wasn't happy about going."

"Did you still have to go?"

"Yes," I replied.

"Pouting rarely helps one get one's way," Gramps said, "In fact, the only person that feels badly is person doing the pouting."

"I certainly felt badly."

"So, tell your mother just once that you aren't happy about going, think of alternatives and then," Gramps continued, "if you know you have to go, choose to go with a smile on your face."

I had to think about that for a while, but what Gramps said did make sense.

"The work around here never ends," Gramps said.

"What do you need done? I could help."

"I like to get a lot of the work done on Wednesdays. I need someone to help me move things when I mow, hold the boats up when I wash them, pick up sticks and whatever else."

"I would be happy to do it, but I have to go to the city on Wednesdays."

"Tom, I'd have to talk to your mother, but maybe you could stay with me on Wednesdays. But you would have to help me. It wouldn't be all fun and games."

"Oh, Gramps, that would break up my week so well. That would be great."

Since that conversation paused, I asked him what I had really come down to ask.

"Would it be okay if I take a boat out?"

"Of course, have fun. Go see if Hank's granddaughter is out," Gramps said with a smile.

That Gramps seems to know everything.

I got in the boat and started rowing, looking at all the houses along the way. As I got closer to Hank's house, I could see her. She was talking with another girl. What should I do? Should I wave? Should I say hi? I just kept rowing. She did look out at me, so I quickly turned away. I decided to go to the east end of the lake and back. I rowed down there, and I found the neighborhood beach, managed by the homeowners in Stan's neighborhood. There were a lot of people laying on the beach and swimming in the water. There were probably people from my school there, so I turned around and rowed back.

I rowed past Hank's house again, but didn't see the girls this time, so I rowed back to Gramps' dock. There were a few speedboats zooming past and few rowboats anchored doing some fishing. I got back and Gramps was throwing horseshoes.

"I've got to practice because both my older daughter and her family and my son and his family are coming out tomorrow, and I am not ready for my son, daughter or son-in-law to beat me," he said with a smile, "Want to play?"

I couldn't resist a game of horseshoes, but it would be tough to beat Gramps. Sure enough, he beat me soundly two games.

I went back home, wanting to tell my mother about Gramps' offer, but she was on the phone. As I waited very impatiently for her to finish, I heard a knock at the door. It was some of the neighbor kids wanting to know if I wanted to play Red Rover. I told them that I would be too big for Red Rover and would win every time, but if they ever wanted to play kickball, I would play. They said they would let me know and went on about their way. All of children in the neighborhood are a little younger than me. I would dominate in kickball against them too.

When my mother got off the phone, I mentioned to her about Gramps' offer. She offered to walk down to the lake with me to talk to Gramps. We walked down to the dock and Gramps was not out. I showed my mother the boats and how I could help Gramps here on Wednesdays. My mother decided to go ring the doorbell while I waited on the dock. Next thing I knew, Gramps and my mother were walking toward the dock.

I heard him say, "Helen, you have a fine young man."

My mother said, "Yes, Dr. Davis, he is very special. I appreciate all the time you spend with him, especially since his father doesn't visit."

I wish she hadn't brought up my father to Gramps. I try not to think about him. It was interesting that she referred to Gramps as Dr. Davis. I don't really see him doing any doctor work, and I have now referred to him as Gramps for a while.

"Tom, do you want to spend Wednesdays with Dr. and Mrs. Davis? Mrs. Davis said she would get you lunch if you worked hard for Dr. Davis."

"Oh, Mom, that would be great. I will work hard here."

"Well, I better go start dinner," said my mother.

"Okay, Mom, I will be up in about 10 minutes."

"Dr. Davis, thank you for everything," she said as she left.

"You have a very nice mother, Tom. You need to treat her well," Gramps said to me.

"I know. She is great, but she talks on the phone a lot."

Gramps said, "Stop down tomorrow. All of the grandchildren will be here."

"Oh, Gramps, Stan invited me to the neighborhood game, but I'll stop down afterwards."

Gramps has three children. His oldest daughter, Mollie, was married with three children: a five-year-old boy, a three-year-old girl and a one-year-old boy. I had played with their oldest son, Todd, a bit. His son, Charlie, was married and had a one-year-old. His youngest daughter, Lucy, was not married at the time and lived in Chicago, where she worked as a consultant. All of his children called him Dad, but called his wife Ruth. Todd calls him Gramps like I did.

"Gramps, why do your children call Mrs. Davis Ruth?"

"Ruth is my third wife. I had all of my children with my first wife. My children's mother lives out in Milford and sees all of my children more than I do."

"Oh, I forgot. You had told me that Mrs. Davis was your third wife. Whatever happened to the second wife?"

"We were married for a few years, but it didn't work out."

"Why not?"

"It was very difficult because she had a teenage son, and she didn't seem to get along my three children. It was very difficult with a blended family."

"Sometimes I think it might be cool to have brothers and sisters, but it would be really different if my mom was to get married. Well, I better head up for dinner. Bye, Gramps," I said and headed off.

—✦—

The next day, I called Stan to see if there was going to be a neighborhood game. He told me to come to Marty's field at about 12:30 p.m., so I rode my bike there along the shoulder of Pontiac Trail. I got there a little early, and there were just a few older boys there who remembered me from the other times I had I played.

The one boy said, "Hey, The Machine, how are you?"

I knew they didn't know my real name, but it was okay.

"Hi, Ed," I responded.

The other boys started wandering in. Joe and Will came walking up, and we acknowledged each other. Bill was also there that day. Then Stan came walking up and threw me a ball.

We picked teams, and I was only the second to last picked. Bill was last. I felt some satisfaction for that. I was on Stan's team again. They let Stan lead off, but I batted last. I didn't get up until the second inning. When we took the field, I ran out to first, and no one challenged me for it. Many of the throws were a little wild, and the field was not in the same shape as the game fields, so it was much more difficult to field the ball on a hop; but I did my best, and I did scoop one throw on the bounce.

In my first at bat, I struck out. I was worried too much about being hit by the pitch from these bigger pitchers. I decided that my second time up, I was really going to concentrate on hitting the ball. This time I hit the first pitch on a line drive, but it was caught by the shortstop for an out. My last time up, I hit the first pitch again, and it was on the ground between the shortstop and the third baseman. The third baseman tried to make the play, but bobbled it, and then threw wildly to first, so I ended up down at second base. It was my first hit in the neighborhood game, and I was starting to fit in, even though all but five of us were at least 11-years-old.

After the game, Stan, Joe, Will and I talked a little. Most of the conversation was about how they were better than some of the older kids, or so they thought. I asked if any of them ever went to their neighborhood beach and they all said they did.

"I have a neighbor who lets me take his rowboats out, and yesterday, I rowed down be the beach."

Joe said, "Hey, we'll look for you this week."

As Joe and Will took off, I told Stan that there were some good-looking girls that I saw out in bikinis when I rowed by. Stan seemed excited and said that he wanted to come out in the boat with me sometime.

I rode my bike back home and asked my mother if I could go jump in the lake.

My mother smiled and said, "Go jump in the lake."

I went down and saw Gramps' daughter, Mollie, and his son-in-law playing with their children in the sand.

Mollie said, "Hey, Todd, there's Tom." Todd came over and asked if I wanted to see his sand castles. I said, "Oh, yes, I'd love to see them," and saw all of his work in the sand, which looked like the work of a five-year-old.

"Todd, I want to go for a swim now," I said.

"Mom, I want to swim with Tom," Todd said.

"I'll watch him," I told Mollie. The water was a little cold, and it didn't take long for Todd to run back out to the beach area. After I got used to the temperature, I started swimming around a little and then came out and dried myself off.

The next morning, I went out to my grandparents. I didn't have much to do out there, so I did some drawing and listened to the Detroit Tiger games with my grandfather. I got pretty good at looking at comics and drawing a good replica. I also did some crossword puzzles from the Dell book that my grandmother got monthly. I found things to do, but really missed talking with other children my age.

On Wednesday, it was my first day of work with Gramps. We started the day by washing the boats. Gramps pulled one at a time up on the dock and turned it over on its side. He gave me a plastic milk container that he had cut the bottom off and told me to scoop water from the lake and throw the water in the boat using the "scoop." I did this, and I could see the dirt and sand and sometimes worms washing out of the boat. We cleaned all of the boats together.

"Tom, that really helps. It is hard to do by myself."

Then Gramps wanted to mow. My job was to pick up sticks, walnuts or anything else in the way. I had fun picking up the walnuts and throwing them like baseballs into the woods. I also helped him move the picnic table to where he had already mowed. It was a fun morning helping him. Around noon, Mrs. Davis called us for lunch, and we ate on his deck. After lunch, he said that I could do what I wanted.

"Gramps, I really want to meet Hank's granddaughter, but I am afraid she might not like me."

"Tom, what is there that's not to like about you? She will be able to see that you are a very handsome young man. She doesn't know anything negative about you. Have you never talked to a girl before?"

"Gramps, sure I've talked to girls, but none that compare to her. She is gorgeous."

"So, Tom, what is the worst that can happen if you say hi to her."

"Well, she might scream, call me names and tell me to get out of there."

"Hmmm, is that what the girls at school do?"

"No," I said with a laugh.

"Is she the only fish in the sea?"

"Of course not."

"So, here's what you do. If she screams and tells you to get out, you leave and come back with some information that you don't have to think about her any longer; she is not nice. That would be good information to have. Now, let's say she says hi back when you say hi. How bad would that be?"

"Oh, that might be bad too because I might say something wrong and feel embarrassed."

"What could you say that is wrong and would embarrass you?"

"I don't know, but I might say something, and she might look at me with disgust."

"That would be good information too, because you don't want girls who look at you with disgust, and you could rule her out. Tom, you have to be yourself. The relationship is only worth it if you can be yourself and she likes you."

"I guess that makes sense."

"Now, Tom, don't try to kiss her when you first meet her. Get to know her a little first and see if she is friendly. Remember the old saying—No Guts, No Glory."

"Okay, Gramps, that makes sense, may I take one of the boats out on the lake?"

"Tom, we just cleaned them!" he said with a smile, "Of course, you can take a boat."

I rowed by Hank's house and no one was out, so I rowed back. I was ready to say something to her, but she wasn't there. Maybe she only comes out on weekends. I would try again on Saturday.

"Hey Jude, don't be afraid.
You were made to go out and get her.
The minute you let her under your skin,
Then you begin to make it better."
— The Beatles (1968)

No Guts, No Glory

After spending a few more days in the city, Saturday was finally here. After the morning shopping and laundry with my mother, I went down and borrowed a boat to try again. Mollie and her family were there, and Todd asked if he could go in the boat with me.

"Todd, not this time," I said, and Todd got so sad I thought he was going to cry. "Okay, Todd, ask your mother and father."

Mollie came up to me and said that I didn't have to take him.

I said, "It's okay. He can come," I said.

Mollie said, "Don't go too far."

What do I do now? I had a five-year-old with me. I couldn't let the dream girl see me with a five-year-old. I decided to row by and at least see if she was out. I rowed close to Hank's and there she was. She looked as fine as ever. Wow. She was out sunbathing. She saw me. I took a deep breath and thought, *No Guts...No Glory*. I waved to her, and to my surprise, she waved back and also seemed to smile. Then Todd waved to her and she waved back at him and smiled too. Wow, this little tyke got as much attention from her as I did. I rowed back to shore and helped Todd out of the boat.

Mollie came up and said, "Now, Todd, what do you say?"

Todd said, "Thank you," and came up and gave me a hug.

I went back home and waited for Mollie and her family to leave and then took the boat out again. This time there was no one out at Hank's house, so I rowed back and went home. I thought about it, and there was nothing negative yet. If nothing else, we had exchanged friendly waves.

On Sunday, I met Stan again for the neighborhood game. I was feeling more comfortable playing in the game. We agreed that I would row down to his beach on Wednesday afternoon and he would be there to meet me.

On Monday, I got my final grades and my room assignment for fifth grade in the mail. I got satisfactory in gym, music and art. I got A's in math, spelling and English. I got an A- in science and a B+ in social studies. I was hoping for all A's, but it was late in the marking period when I had started to make more of an effort. I would have to make getting all A's my goal for fifth grade.

On Wednesday, I helped Gramps with his work, had lunch and then took the boat out. No one was out at Hank's, but I kept going down to Stan's neighborhood beach. As I approached, I saw Stan by the shore, so I pulled the boat up on shore, and Stan and I sat on the beach and looked around at the girls. We had fun joking around and looking at people. I saw a few people I knew from school, and they came up and talked to us. The best part was finding out that Stan would be in the same class as me for the fifth grade. We had a fun time together. After a few hours, I got back in the boat and rowed home. We started doing this every

Wednesday. This one day a week really helped to solidify our friendship.

—◆—

On Saturday, I headed out again to look for the dream girl at Hank's house. I called her the dream girl since I still didn't know her name. She was there again with two friends this time. I waved and all three girls waved back.

"Hi, I'm Tom, from down the lake."

I blew it already. I'm from down the lake. She must think that I am a fish. What a stupid thing to say.

The dream girl asked, "Where is your little brother today?"

I smiled and said, "He's not my brother. He's the neighbor's grandson. Do you live here?"

"No," she said, "This is my grandparents' house, but my parents bring me and sometimes my friends out on weekends."

"What is your name?"

"Teresa...and these are my friends, Mary and Donna."

"It's nice meeting all of you. I hope to see around."

"Nice finally meeting you, Tom. Come by and say hi again," Teresa said.

As I rowed on, I could hear the girls giggling.

I rowed back and tried to assess the situation. Did I say anything really stupid? I think I was okay. I wasn't planning on the other girls being there. Well, at least I got her name. Wow, every time I see her, she looks better and better. She had a really nice tan, big eyes and there was something about that long silky hair that I really liked. She didn't scream and tell me to get lost, so the worst-case scenario didn't happen. I couldn't wait to see her again.

The following Saturday, she wasn't there when I rowed by. I had waited all week. What a disappointment! I felt sad that day and didn't feel like doing anything. I finally decided I would just have to try again the next weekend. I hoped that she wasn't trying to avoid me.

The following Saturday was June 29th, so I took the boat out again and this time she was out by herself. I yelled out, "Hi, Teresa!"

"Hi, Tom!"

She had remembered my name. That seemed like a good sign. I rowed a little closer.

"Would you like to come for a boat ride?"

I was so proud of myself. What a smooth line!

"I better not," she said, "my mother wouldn't like it if I went out without asking someone, but you can pull your boat up on shore, and we can talk for awhile."

I rowed up and pulled the boat up on shore. There was an extra chair, and she asked me to sit down.

"So Tom, you live down the lake a little. It must be great to live on the lake all year round. I live in the city," Teresa said.

I knew that saying that I lived down the lake was stupid. Maybe I could recover from this like I did when I called the umpire crazy.

"Actually, Teresa, I don't live right on the lake, but I walk to my neighbor's house who does live on the lake. I help him with chores and he lets me swim and take his boats out."

I wondered if I just lost value because I don't live on the lake.

"What grade are you in?"

She is still asking questions, so maybe I did recover.

"I am going into fifth grade at Twin Beach. What about you?"

"I will be in fifth grade at Riley," she said as she smiled, "Riley is an upper elementary school. I used to go to Rosedale."

"Upper Elementary?" I asked, confused.

"Yes, in Livonia, we go to lower elementary through the fourth grade, so I was attending Rosedale, and then upper elementary for fifth and sixth," she said smiling again.

"Twin Beach is kindergarten through sixth, so I have now been there for 5 years and have two years to go."

I had no idea that all elementary schools didn't have the same grade levels.

"Do you like school?" I asked, scraping for something to keep the conversation going.

"Yes, I do. What about you?"

"Yes, I do too," I said, "So what is there to do in Livonia?"

Oh, no! Why would I ask that? It sounded negative.

"I am in the community theatre and choir. It's a lot of fun. What about you?"

"I play baseball. I'm a first baseman. We did okay this year. I hit a grand slam homerun to beat the undefeated team on the last day of the season."

I couldn't wait to get that out.

"Wow," she said, "That is impressive. Do you want to meet my parents? I think if they met you, they might be okay with me going for a boat ride? I'll be right back."

Meet the parents? I was just trying to get a kiss from the dream girl. Where is this going?

Teresa returned from the house with her mother, father, grandmother and grandfather. She introduced everyone to me. I remembered to shake hands with all of the adults as they were introduced.

"So, where do you live?" her grandfather asked.

"I live on Pontiac Trail with my mother. We are good friends with Ray Davis, who goes to our church. He owns the boats and lets me borrow them."

"I know Ray. He's a doctor. He's a good man," her grandfather said. "You can take a little ride, but we want to watch you, so stay in our sight," her mother said.

"Okay," she said, and we walked down and she got in the boat.

I pushed the boat off and began to row. We rowed around talking and smiling. I wanted to tell her how pretty she was, but Gramps had warned me about doing too much too early. After a little ride, I took her back to shore. Her parents and grandparents were waiting for her. I don't think they took their eyes off of us the entire time.

She got out of the boat and thanked me. I didn't want to wear out my welcome, so I decided to get in the boat and head back.

Then Teresa asked her parents, "Would it be okay if Tom comes over on Thursday to watch the fireworks with us?"

Thursday was Independence Day and was always celebrated on the Fourth of July with fireworks. President Johnson had decided not to make this one of the Monday holidays starting in 1971.

Her grandmother said, "Sure, we cook out, so come around 7:00."

Then her mother said, "Bring your mother too. I'd like to meet her."

My mother? Wow, this really was a "meet the parents."

I said, "Thank you. I will check with my mother."

Her grandmother wrote her name and number on a piece of paper, gave it to me and said, "Have your mother call me, please."

I said that I would and headed out.

What a day! What a very special day! Teresa was so very special!

The Baseball Bat

"Well, you've got your diamonds
and you've got your pretty clothes
and the chauffeur drives your car.
You let everybody know.
But don't play with me
'Cause you're playing with fire."
— The Rolling Stones (1965)

Fireworks

My mother had called and made arrangements for us to visit with Teresa and her family on the Fourth of July. My mother made a potato salad and cookies to bring to the gathering. It was little strange driving to the front of their house, since I had only seen her from the back of the house. Wow, I had dreamed about this girl, and so far, she was everything I had hoped she would be. I just couldn't get over how beautiful she was and how nice she was to me. It was probably best she hadn't seen me at school and how mad I got at times. I didn't want her to see me like that. I wanted her to see me as nice. I had asked my mother not to say anything negative about me, since I had heard her on the phone many times talking about me and my struggles.

We arrived at the house. Even though it was walking distance, my mother still wanted to drive. Teresa took me to the back yard, and we talked as we looked out at the lake. My mother seemed to be hitting it off well with her parents. I found out that she was an only child too, and that her father was actually her stepfather, to whom her mother has been married for five years. The more we talked, the more we found that we had in common.

Teresa and I laughed and smiled the entire time. We told a few jokes. I did draw the line and didn't tell her how to catch a bear; I thought I should keep it clean.

The fireworks were shot off from Stan's neighborhood beach, and we could see them well from where we were at her grandfather's house. It was dark, and I thought about trying to kiss Teresa, but there were too many people around. We did sit right next to each other the entire time and our legs touched at times. After the fireworks were over, we left, but I asked Teresa when she would be out again. She asked her parents and they told her probably Saturday, July 20th, so I told her I would try to see her then.

The following Wednesday, I again helped Gramps in the morning and had lunch before rowing down to look for Stan. In the morning while we were working, I decided to ask Gramps again about anger.

"Gramps, so tell me everything I should do to help me control my anger. I really want to make sure I control anger now that I have a special lady."

"Tom, first we have to agree that anger can be controlled. We tried to prove this by saying that if you were offered a large sum of money, you would be able to stay calm and not get angry by focusing on the money. Do you believe anger can be controlled through thinking?"

"I do, Gramps. I have been successful thinking in ways to control my anger at times, but I want to do better. I want to reduce the times I get angry. I have a dream girl now, and I don't want to lose her."

Gramps smiled. "The second step is deciding that your life would be better without anger. You just told me you have a goal to not get angry in front of your dream girl. Do you not want to get angry on the bus, at school, with your mother?"

"All anger does is make everything worse for me. I want to handle the challenges of life by staying calm and thinking with my..."

"...Your frontal cortex? Your decision making part of the brain?"

"Yes, my frontal cortex, so that I can make good decisions."

"Tom, will you want to teach someone a lesson or intimidate someone?"

"Gramps, I am going to do my best to not get angry, but also to sternly speak up for myself when appropriate."

"Great. I think that will work well for you."

"Now for step three, we decided that not all of your thoughts were true thoughts, right?"

"Yes, we decided that if I think something is awful, it isn't because being hit over the head with a baseball bat is awful. Most situations are less than awful."

"Very good. Also, what did we decide if we think we can't stand something?"

"It is better to think that we don't like something, but we can stand it because we have stood a similar situation before."

"Tom, you could be teaching this. Now, how should we expect people to act and think?"

"This is a hard one for me, Gramps. I know I can't expect people to be nice like me. I can't expect people to act like me or to think like me. I have to expect people to act and think like themselves, even if they are rude."

"Tom, you're right. Remember, we don't have to like how people act, but we should expect them to act like themselves. Now, so far the only appraisal system that we set up was either I don't like it or it is awful. Now for step four. Sometimes, it is helpful if we assign a value from one to ten to something we don't like. For instance, we may not like someone clearing their throat while we are taking a test, but that would be appraised as a one. Now, you know what a ten is, right?"

"Yes, someone who's putting my life in danger, like trying to beat me with a baseball bat."

"So, we have a one and a ten. What if your mother tells you to clean your room while you are engaged in a television show?"

"I really wouldn't like that."

"However, Tom, that is a three and you would not want to get angry. What if someone calls you a name? What if someone kicks your seat?"

"I don't like either of those. Neither of those is a one or a ten."

"Tom, we will call those situations I just mentioned an appraisal of a five. So, what I would like you to do is not get angry at anything six or below."

"So, I can get angry for a seven. What would a seven be?"

"Let's say a seven would be a situation when someone pushes you and yells in your face. If a fourth grader got angry about this, I don't think it would surprise a lot of people. I think you will do well this year to not get angry at appraisals of one through six."

"Gramps, I am going into the fifth grade this year, but I understand your point. I will do my best. What is the next step?"

"Step five is keeping a sense of humor."

"A sense of humor? Like when we tell jokes?"

"Something like that, only keeping a sense of humor when someone does something we don't like, and laughing to ourselves that they aren't as nice a person as us."

"Gramps, that's funny."

"Yes, it is. Keeping your sense of humor and having fun will help keep you from getting angry. There are two more steps to remember. Step six is to remember your goals and keep reminding yourself of them. You accomplished your goals in baseball by working hard. Now you need to keep working on your goal of controlling your emotions. This takes hard work too. Tell yourself this goal often."

"My goal is to not get angry, not get suspended, to have friends and to not get in trouble."

"Keep reminding yourself of these goals every day."

"You mentioned one more step?"

"The final step is to understand that we are not perfect, and we make mistakes. If you get angry at some point, understand that it happened, accept it and don't beat yourself up over it. Tom, none of us are perfect."

I smiled.

"Gramps, I used to think I was perfect, and at 9-years-old, that I knew more than anyone else. You taught me some valuable lessons that I did not learn in school. I really appreciate it."

"Tom, so do you know everything now?"

"Gramps, I have a plan to control my anger that I hope works most of the time, but I have a feeling I still have a lot more to learn about life."

We both smiled.

"Tom, you have enough to think about for now, but we will talk many more times about other life lessons."

"Gramps, that would be great."

"So, when are you going to see that dream girl again?"

"Hopefully, on July 20th."

I got in a boat and headed off to find Stan. I found him and we hung out on the beach. Stan was talking about a guy going into sixth grade that was a really good first baseman. I couldn't believe he was talking about this, and I felt hurt. I tried to appraise the situation like Gramps had taught me. I decided it was a two and my goal was to keep Stan as a friend. I was able to speak calmly to Stan.

"Stan, I know this guy is good, but I want to be better than him someday."

"Tom, someday I know you will be a lot better than him. By the way, I want you to play on my football team this fall. We can go sign up together. Football will be so much fun."

By remaining calm, I was able to say what I thought about what Stan had said and kept a sense of humor about it. If I hadn't said anything, I would have held on to it, but I felt better after Stan affirmed confidence in me. Football! I hadn't really thought about it, but now that I was friends with Stan, I was excited about this sport too.

On Saturday, July 20th, I rowed the boat by the house, and Teresa was outside sunbathing. She was so beautiful in anything she would have been wearing, but the bikini made her even more attractive. I pulled the boat on shore and we talked for a couple hours. I told her that I had to go to my grandparents' house, but would see her again soon. I rowed back and felt so elated from talking to her. I couldn't help but think that in one year, I had gone from an angry kid to having the girl of my dreams in Teresa and the most popular and athletic boy in the school, Stan, as my new best friend.

When I got to my grandparents' house, my grandfather told me that the Detroit Tigers had lost, but they were still in first place. He told me about the previous game where they were down 4-2 and got three runs in the bottom of the ninth inning on a homerun hit by shortstop Tom Matchick.

"Wow, there is something about the name Tom and snatching victory away from defeat," my grandfather said with a laugh.

My grandfather went on to tell me that Denny McLain was now 18-2 on the year, and that he might have 20 wins before the end of July. As it turned out, McLain won his 21st game on July 31st and went on to win 31 games in the 1968 regular season. My grandfather heard some beats on his radio and then turned up the song that was playing.

"We're all behind our baseball team.
Go get 'em Tigers.
World Series bound and pickin' up steam.
Go get 'em Tigers."

I learned the song and had fun singing it.

I continued to work with Gramps every Wednesday and went to see Stan afterwards. It was always a good time. I continued to look for Teresa every Saturday. I saw her again on August 3rd and we laughed and had fun.

When it was almost time for me to go, she looked at me seriously and said, "Tom, I have really enjoyed seeing you this summer. You are so handsome, athletic and fun. I really like you a lot."

I looked at her and said, "Teresa, you are the most beautiful girl and so much fun. I like you a lot too."

I had never kissed a girl before, but just then she leaned toward me and pecked my lips with hers. It only lasted a second, but it was so special to me. We both said our goodbyes and hoped to see each other soon.

I rowed by her grandparents' house every Saturday in August, but never saw her out. I guess I would have to wait until next summer. I was sad each Saturday I did not see her, but wanted to focus on getting all A's, keeping friendships, and controlling my anger, and I decided I was going to work hard on those goals in the fifth grade. When I thought about Teresa, I tried to think happy thoughts and not about how much I missed her. If I did start to miss her, I used one of Gramps' thinking techniques. I told myself that it could be worse. Someone could be hitting me over the head with a baseball bat.

References &
Recommended Readings

Ellis, Albert. 1975. *A Guide to Rational Living*. Chatsworth, CA: Wilshire Book Company.

Ellis, Albert. 1997. *How to Control Your Anger Before It Controls You*. New York: Kensington Publishing Corp.

About the Author

James Shaw, PsyD, was born in Pontiac, Michigan and lived in the metropolitan Detroit area through high school. He is now a licensed psychologist and clinical assistant professor at The Ohio State University Wexner Medical Center Family Practice.

Made in the USA
Charleston, SC
18 October 2013